A STOLEN KISS

Valerian looked down at her, seeing the adorable pout that had appeared on her enticingly pink lips, and swallowed hard.

He had to retain the knowledge that she was little more than a child.

He had to remind himself that he was a man of the world, an honorable man, and knew better than to steal a kiss from an innocent.

He had to remember that he, although so much older than she, and the possessor of graying temples, was still a reasonably young man of five and thirty, and not nearly ready to settle down and start his nursery.

He had to keep it clear in his mind that—"Oh, the hell with it!"

Valerian quickly took Allegra's chin between his fingers. "Imp," he said, his voice husky. "If you think I'm going to ask your permission for this first, you're fair and far out!" So saying, he lowered his head to hers and allowed himself to succumb to the sanity-destroying attraction of her moist, pouting mouth.

Kasey Michaels is the *New York Times* and *USA Today* bestselling author of more than sixty books. She has won the Romance Writers of America RITA Award and the *Romantic Times* Career Achievement Award for her historical romances set in the Regency era, and also writes contemporary romances for Silhouette and Harlequin Books.

The Chaotic
Miss Crispino

HARLEQUIN®

TORONTO • NEW YORK • LONDON
AMSTERDAM • PARIS • SYDNEY • HAMBURG
STOCKHOLM • ATHENS • TOKYO • MILAN • MADRID
PRAGUE • WARSAW • BUDAPEST • AUCKLAND

To my niece and godchild, Lisa Scheidler Johnston, who is as chaotically wonderful as Allegra, and just as beautiful!

ISBN 0-373-51185-X

THE CHAOTIC MISS CRISPINO

Visit us at www.eHarlequin.com

Printed in U.S.A.

CHAPTER ONE

VALERIAN FITZHUGH stood before the narrow window he had pushed open in the vain hope that some of the stale, dank air trapped within the small room might be so accommodating as to exchange places with a refreshing modicum of the cooler, damp breeze coming in off the moonlit Arno.

Both the river that divided the city and the lofty dome of the Cattedrale di Santa Maria del Fiore were vaguely visible from Fitzhugh's vantage point, although that particular attribute could not be thought to serve as any real consolation for his reluctant presence in the tumbledown *pensione*.

Florence, birthplace of the Renaissance, had been one of Valerian's favorite cities when he had visited Italy during his abbreviated Grand Tour some sixteen years previously, although his youthful adventures had come to an abrupt halt when the brief Treaty of Amiens had been shattered. So it was with a willing heart that he had begun charting his current three-year-long return to the Continent in Brussels the very morning after Napoleon had been vanquished forever at Waterloo.

Touching a hand to his breast pocket, Valerian felt again the much-folded, much-traveled sheets of paper that had led him, two and one half years into his journey—and not without considerable trouble—to this small, dark, damp room on quite the most humble street in Florence.

It was damnably wearying, being an honorable man, but Valerian could not in good conscience turn his back on the plea from Lord Dugdale (his late father's oldest and dearest friend) that had finally caught up with him at his hotel in Venice—and the crafty Denny Dugdale, never shy when it came to asking for assistance, had known it.

So here Valerian stood, at five minutes past midnight on a wet, wintry night just six days after the ringing in of the year of 1818, waiting for the baron's difficult-to-run-to-ground granddaughter to return to her pitifully mean second-story room in a decrepit *pensione* so that he could take a reluctant turn at playing fairy godmother.

"...and chaperon...and traveling companion," Valerian said aloud, sighing.

He stole a moment from his surveillance of the entrance to the *pensione* beneath the window to look once more around the small room, his gaze taking in the sagging rope bed, the single, near-gutted candle stuck to a metal dish, the small, chipped dresser, and one worn leather satchel that looked as if it had first been used during the time of Columbus.

"One can only hope the chit knows the English word for soap." A second long-suffering sigh escaped him as he turned back to the window once more to continue his vigil.

"Chi é? Che cosa cera?"

Valerian hesitated momentarily as the low, faintly husky female voice asked him who he was and what he was looking for. He stiffened in self-reproach because he hadn't heard her enter the room, then a second later remembered that he had glanced away from the entrance for a minute, probably just as she had come down the narrow alley to the *pensione.*

Slowly turning to face her through the dimness that the flickering candle did little to dissipate, a benign, non-threatening smile deliberately pasted on his lean, handsome face, he bowed perfunctorily and replied, "*Il mio nome é* Valerian Fitzhugh, Signorina Crispino. *Parla inglese*, I sincerely pray?"

The girl took two more daring steps into the room, her arms akimbo, her hot gaze raking him up and down as if measuring his capacity for mayhem. "*Sì. Capisco.* That is to say, yes, Signor Fitzhugh, I speak English," she said at last, her accent faint but delightful, "which makes it that much easier for me to order you to vacate my room—*presto!*"

Instead of obeying her, Valerian leaned against the window frame and crossed his arms in front of his chest. His relaxed pose seemed to prompt her to take yet another two steps into the room, bringing her—considering the size of the chamber—within three feet of her uninvited guest.

"You speak, signore, but do you hear? I said you are to leave my room!"

"Do not be afraid. I am not here to harm you, signorina," he told her, believing her aggressive action resulted more from bravado than from fearlessness.

Her next words quickly disabused him of that notion. "Harm me? Ha! As if you could. These walls are like paper, signore. One scream from me and the whole household would be in here. Now, go away! Whatever position you are offering me, I must tell you I have no choice but to refuse it. I leave Firenze tonight."

"Position? I don't follow you, signorina. But, be that as it may, aren't you even the least bit interested in how I came to know your name?"

"Such a silly question." She threw back her head in an eloquent gesture of disdain at his blatant admission of ignorance. "Everyone knows me, signore. I am *famosa*—famous!"

Valerian's lips quivered in amusement. "Is that so? And modest too, into the bargain. However, if you don't mind, we'll pass over that for the moment and get on to the reason for my presence here."

She sighed, her impatience obvious as she rolled her eyes upward. "Very well, if you insist. But I have not the time for a long story."

Valerian spoke quickly, sensing that what he had to tell her was rough ground he would wisely get across as rapidly as possible. "I am not here to employ you. I have been sent here by your English grandfather, to fetch you home. How wonderful that your mother taught you her native tongue. It will simplify things once you are in Brighton. Excuse me, but what is that smell? There are so many vile odors in this room, but this one is new, and particularly unlovely."

"Smell? How dare you!" Her hands came up as if

she were contemplating choking him, then dropped to her sides. "*Mia madre?* I don't understand. What do you know of my dearest *madre* signore? Or of my terrible *nonno,* who broke her poor heart?"

The hands came up again—for the urge to remove Valerian from the room had overcome her temporary curiosity. "*Magnifico,* signore! You almost deflected me, didn't you? But no, I shall not be distracted. I have no time, no interest. It's those terrible Timoteos. I must pack. I must leave here, at once. As soon as I eat!"

So saying, she reached into the low-cut bodice of the white peasant blouse Valerian had been eyeing with some interest—Miss Crispino might be a mere dab of a girl, the top of her head not quite reaching his shoulders, but her breasts were extremely ample— so that his disappointment could be easily assumed as he watched her retract her hand, holding up a foot-long string of small sausages.

His left eyebrow lifted a fraction, his disappointment tempered by the realization that the blouse remained remarkably well filled. "At least now I know the origin of that unpleasant odor I mentioned earlier. How devilish ingenious of you, Signorina Crispino. I should never have thought to keep sausages in my shirt."

She waited until she had filled her mouth with a lusty bite of the juicy meat before replying, waving the string of sausages in front of his face, "You never would have thought to steal them from the stall on the corner either, Signor Fitzhugh, from the look of you. But then you don't give the impression of someone who has ever known hunger.''

"You filched the sausages?"

She took another bite, again thrusting the remainder of the string up near his face. "Ah! I congratulate you, signore. You have, as we say, discovered America—asked the obvious. Of course I filched them. I am a terrible person—a terrible, desperate person.''

"Really." Valerian remained an unimpressed audience.

"This filching; it is a temporary necessity." She stepped closer, the nearly overpowering aroma of garlic stinging Valerian's eyes and aristocratic nostrils. "But I do not sell my favors on the street for food— or for anything! I make my own way, in my own way. You can tell *il nonno,* my grandfather, that when you see him—which will be in Hell, if my prayers to the Virgin should be answered. Now get out of my way. I must pack.''

She turned to pick up the scuffed leather case but was halted by the simple application of Valerian's hand to her upper arm. "Oh, no, you don't," he commanded softly. "I have wasted nearly a month chasing you from one small *città* to another. I have stood here patiently and watched as you displayed a lack of good manners that would have distressed your dear mother to tears. Now you, signorina, are going to hear me out.

"Duggy—your grandfather—is dying, and he wants to ease his way through Heaven's gate by leaving his fortune to his only grandchild. You, Signorina Crispino, more's the pity, are that grandchild. I am here to offer my assistance in returning you to Brighton, to''—he could not resist a glance at the bodice of her blouse—''the bosom of your family.''

''Basta!'' Miss Crispino turned her head to one side and very deliberately spat on the scarred wooden floor. ''Enough! I spit on my grandfather! I spit on my mother's family—seed, sprout, and flower!''

''How utterly charming,'' Valerian remarked, unmoved. ''Your aunt Agnes will positively adore you, I'm sure—once she has recovered from her faint. Now, if you have finally done with the overblown Italian theatrics, perhaps you will take a moment to listen to what I have to say. Duggy may have disowned your mother for marrying your father, but he has lived to repent the action. He's dying, signorina, and he wants to make amends for his sins.

''If you can't bring yourself to forgive him, perhaps you can screw yourself up to the notion of inheriting every last groat the man has collected over the years. It's not an inconsiderable sum, I assure you.''

She pulled her arm free of his grasp and picked up the satchel. ''You begin to interest me, but *belle parole non pascolano I gatti,* signore—fine words don't feed cats. How do I know my fickle grandfather won't have had yet another change of his dark heart by the time I reach this place, this Brighton?''

Valerian answered truthfully, his job done—at least in his mind—now that he had delivered Lord Dugdale's message. ''You don't know that, I suppose. It is also true that a woman—even one of your obvious, um, *talents*— would perhaps find it difficult to make her living in England alone. So, as you seem to be

getting on so swimmingly here in Italy, I can see that
you might be reluctant to trade all this luxury for the
chance at a fortune.''

"You make fun of me, signore; you doubt me. But
I do not care. My *talent* it is not inconsiderable.'' She
busily pulled various bits of clothing from the dresser
drawers and flung them into the open satchel. "I in-
herited it from my magnificent *papà*, who was the
master of his age! I am a most famous *cantante*— an
opera singer—and I am in great demand!''

Valerian watched as she unearthed several rather
intimate items of apparel and wadded them into a ball
before stuffing them into the satchel, doing her best
to keep her back between the undergarments and Valerian's eyes.

"Really? Then I stand corrected,'' he remarked
coolly, peeking over her shoulder to see that her
hands were shaking. "But I have been in Italy for
two months. Isn't it strange that I have not heard of
you?''

"I have been resting, signore,'' she said, wincing,
for the term was one that many singers used to explain why they were unemployed. She could find
work every night of the week if she wanted to—if it
weren't for those horrible Timoteos, curse them all to
everlasting damnation!

"It's my throat,'' she lied quickly. "It is strained.
But I will be performing again soon—very soon—in
Roma.''

"Which of course also explains your rush to quit
this charming *pensione* in the middle of the night,''
Valerian said agreeably, wishing he was not interested

in knowing why the girl was in such a hurry, or why her hands were trembling. "I should have guessed it. Perhaps you will allow me to transport you safely to the nearest coaching inn?"

She pulled a length of rope from the drawer, using it to tie the satchel closed, as the clasp had come to grief months earlier, not by accident but merely by rotting away with age. She hefted the thing onto her shoulder. "You'd do that, signore? You aren't going to press me about accompanying you to England?"

Valerian shrugged indifferently. "If you're asking if I'm about to carry you off will-nilly against your wishes, I fear you have badly mistaken your man. I've been most happily traveling across Europe in a long-delayed Grand Tour of sorts, and interrupting it to play ape-leader to a reluctant heiress was not part of my agenda. No, Signorina Crispino, I have wasted enough time with this project. It is time I continue my journey."

She looked at him carefully, piercingly, for the first time, taking in his well-cut, modish clothes, his tall, leanly muscular frame, and the healthy shock of thick black hair accented by snow-white "angel wings" at the temples—although they didn't make him look the least angelic, but rather dashing in a disturbing sort of way.

"*Naturalmente*. If I had looked harder, I should have seen more. Like overcooked pasta, Signor Fitzhugh, you are appealing to the eye, but upon further investigation, can be quickly dismissed as unpalatable, being soft at the center and rather mushy. Now, if you will excuse me?"

Valerian merely bowed, her verbal barb seemingly having no effect on him.

Just as she turned for the door it crashed open, banging loudly against the inside wall and nearly ripping free of its rusted hinges. A heartbeat later a large masculine shape appeared in the doorway. *"Ha!"* the shape bellowed, his roar one of triumph as he caught sight of Signorina Crispino.

His elation quickly dissipated, however, when he espied Valerian, who was once more standing near the window. The man turned to Signorina Crispino, asking, *"Chi?"* even as he extracted a small metal mallet from his breeches pocket, raised it above his head, and advanced in Valerian's direction.

"Bernardo, no! Un momento, per favore!" Allegra made to grab at the man's arm, but he flicked her away as if she were an annoying fly. "Signor Fitzhugh, be careful! He is crazy and won't listen to me! I can't stop him! You must run! *Bernardo farà polpette di tuo*—he will make meatballs out of you!"

"Sì, the little meatballs!" Bernardo concurred in heavily accented English, grinning his appreciation of that description of what he and his little mallet would soon be doing to Valerian, the weapon gleaming dully in the faint light.

Valerian was not by nature a timid man, far from it, nor was he incapable of protecting himself. He just, frankly, wasn't in the mood for a fist fight with a man no taller than he was but twice as muscular and at least five years younger. Was this Bernardo even real? No human should be so beautiful—at least not a man.

Besides, the fellow was armed, and that didn't really seem fair.

He decided to even up the odds a bit. Reaching into his breast pocket, Valerian pulled out a small pistol and pointed it at Bernardo, halting him in mid-attack.

"Call off your dog, signorina," he ordered amicably enough, "before I am forced to place a small hole between the eyebrows on his pretty face. And I so abhor violence."

Signorina Crispino lifted her slim shoulders in an eloquent shrug before turning her back on the pair of them and heading for the door. "And why would I warn him, signore?" she called over her shoulder. "Shoot him, *per favore*. You will be doing me a great service. *Addio,* Bernardo."

The pistol wavered, only slightly and only for a moment, as Valerian watched the girl go, leaving him standing almost toe to toe with Bernardo, who was jabbering at him in something that sounded like Italian, but not like any Italian the Englishman was accustomed to hearing.

Now what was Valerian going to do? He certainly wasn't about to shoot the man—he had never really considered doing that—but with that option lost to him, the metal mallet did once more make the two of them an unmatched pair.

"Signorina Crispino—come back here!" he yelled as Bernardo growled low in his throat, raising the mallet another fraction as if unafraid of either Valerian or the weapon in his hand. "I warn you, I shan't hang alone. Come back here at once or I'll tell the authorities that you ordered the killing!''

Her head reappeared around the doorjamb. ''You English,'' she said scathingly. ''What a bloodless lot. You can't even put a hole through a man who is trying to bash in your skull. And as for honor—why, you have none!''

''It's not that, signorina,'' Valerian corrected her urbanely. ''It's just that a prolonged sojourn in one of your quaint Italian prisons until explanations can be made ranks very low on my agenda. I've heard the plumbing in those places is not of the best. Now, are you going to call this incarnation of an ancient Roman god off or not? I'm afraid his notion of the Italian language and mine do not coincide, and I don't wish to insult him further with some verbal misstep.''

Shrugging yet again, Signorina Crispino walked over to Bernardo and gave him a swift kick in the leg in order to gain his attention. *"Bernardo, tu hai il cervello di una gallina! Vai al diavolo!"*

''Oh, that's lovely, that is,'' Valerian interposed. ''Although I hesitate to point this out, I could have told Bernardo here that he has the brain of a chicken. *I* also could have told him to go lose himself somewhere. Can't you just tell your lover that I'm harmless—that I'm a friend of your grandfather's?''

''My lover! You insult me!'' she exploded, throwing down the satchel. ''As if that were true—could ever be true!'' Her hands drawn into tight fists, she wildly looked about the small room in search of a weapon, seizing on the lighted candle that stood in a heavy pewter base, not knowing whom to hit with it first, Bernardo or Valerian.

Bernardo, who seemed to have tired of staring down the short barrel of the pistol, and who did not take kindly to the insults Signorina Crispino had thrown at him, took the decision out of her hands by the simple means of turning to her, his smile wide in his innocently handsome face. "Allegra—*mi amore!*"

"Ah, how affecting. The Adonis loves you," Valerian said, earning himself a cutting glance from Allegra.

"*Fermata!* Stop it—both of you!" she warned tightly just as Valerian's pistol came down heavily on the side of Bernardo's head and the man crumpled into a heap at her feet. She looked from Valerian to Bernardo's inert form and then back at Valerian once again. "*Bene,* signore. *Molto bene.* I thought you said you abhorred violence."

Valerian replaced the pistol in his pocket. "I have learned a new saying since coming to Italy, Signorina Allegra: *'Quando sé in ballo, bisogna ballare.'* When at a dance, one must dance. Your Bernardo left me no choice. Thank you for coming back, by the way. It was cursed good of you."

He looked down at the unconscious Bernardo. "I didn't really wish to hit him. It was like taking a hatchet to a Michelangelo. I don't think I've ever seen such a pretty face."

"Behind which resides the most bricklike brain in the good Lord's nature," Allegra retorted, giving Bernardo's inert figure a small kick. "He speaks some

English, you know, but it goes straight out of his head—pouf!—when he has to do more than stand up straight and be handsome. *Sogni d'oro, Bernardo*—golden dreams to you. Now, Signor Fitzhugh, I suggest we take ourselves out of this place before he rouses, for Bernardo has a very hard head and won't sleep for long.''

Valerian bent to retrieve her satchel. ''A praiseworthy resolution, signorina. But I must ask again, in light of what has just happened—will you please reconsider accompanying me back to England? This Bernardo fellow doesn't seem like the sort to give up and go away. He has been chasing you, hasn't he? That's the reason you have been so difficult to locate—you've been on the run.''

''I've been avoiding Bernardo, *sì*,'' Allegra bit her bottom lip, considering how much and what she wished to tell him. ''Bernardo has convinced himself he wants to marry me, and won't take no for an answer. And he won't give up; I can see that now. Yes, I think I might go along with you, although it won't be a simple matter to cross over the border.'' She took the satchel from Valerian's unresisting fingers. ''I have no passport, signore, so we will have to sneak out of the country. It may take some time.''

''Valerian Fitzhugh forced to sneak out of Italy? What a lovely picture that conjures,'' Valerian remarked, closing the door behind them as they quit the room. ''But I do have some friends located in Naples at the moment. We should find help there. It would mean a few nights on the road.''

Allegra nodded once, accepting this. ''Very well,

signore. But I must warn you—I shan't sleep with you!''

Valerian looked her up and down, seeing her clearly for the first time in the brighter light of the hallway. She was wildly beautiful in her coarse peasant dress, this Allegra Crispino, her ebony hair a tousled profusion of midnight glory as it tumbled around her face and below her shoulders. Her eyes shone like quality sapphires against her fair skin, and her features were appealingly petite and well formed. Almost as well formed as her delightful body.

However, she was also none too clean, her feet were bare, and the smell of garlic hung around her like a shroud. ''My hopes, signorina, are quite cut up, I assure you,'' he said at last, tongue-in-cheek, ''but I would not think of despoiling Duggy's granddaughter. Your virtue is safe with me.''

For now, he concluded silently, still holding out some faint hope for the restorative powers of soap and water.

THEY HAD QUIT the *pensione* and were nearing the corner of the small side street and Valerian's waiting carriage when two large men jumped out of the shadows of a nearby building to block their way.

His eyes on the men, Valerian asked softly, ''Friends of yours? I sense a pattern forming, signorina.''

''Alberto! Giorgio!'' Allegra exploded in exasperation as Valerian's small pistol quickly came into view once more, the sight of the weapon stopping the men in their tracks before they could do any damage.

"Am I never to be shed of these dreadful, thick-skulled Timoteos?"

Valerian eyed the two men warily as the coachman, who had seen his master's dilemma, hopped from the seat and came up behind them, an ugly but effective blunderbuss clutched in his hands. "Lord luv a duck, sir, but these sure are big 'uns. Oi told yer there'd be trouble in this part of town. Yer wants ter drop 'em? Oi gots the one on the right."

"Not yet, Tweed, but I thank you most sincerely for the offer," Valerian answered. "Signorina Crispino—tell your hulking friends here to be on their way, *per favore,* or it will be the worse for them."

Allegra immediately launched into a stream of colloquial, Italian like none Valerian had ever heard before, the whole of her speech punctuated by exaggerated arm movements and eloquent gestures that made him momentarily wonder, were her hands ever to be tied behind her back, if she would then be rendered speechless.

Giorgio and Alberto twisted their heads about to see Tweed—the man extremely unprepossessing with his small stature, skinny frame, and black patch that covered his right eye. His blunderbuss, however—the barrel of which was steadily pointing first toward one of them and then at the other—was another matter, and the two Timoteos exchanged speculative glances before turning back to look at Allegra.

"Bernardo?" Giorgio questioned worryingly. *"Dove posso trovare Bernardo? M-m-morto?"*

Allegra jabbed Valerian in the ribs with her elbow. "Isn't that wonderul? Giorgio thinks his brother is dead. Look at him, Signor Fitzhugh—his knobby knees quiver like the strings of a plucked violin. What shall I tell him? Shall I tell him you killed his brother? That you made meatballs of his pretty face? It would serve him right, *capisci,* for what they have tried to do to me.''

''You're more than usually animated when you're bloodthirsty, signorina, but I don't think I can allow you to do that,'' Valerian answered, watching as a single large tear ran down Giorgio's cheek. The young man's features were almost as perfect as his brother's, although the youth standing next to him, Alberto, must have been hiding behind the *porta* when the family good looks had been handed out, for he was as ugly as Bernardo and Giorgio were beautiful. ''Tell me, just for the sake of intellectual curiosity—are all three of them brothers?''

She shook her head. ''Alberto is a *cugino,* a cousin. His mother must have been frightened by a *tarantola,* don't you think?''

''A tarantula? He is as darkly hairy as a spider, Signorina Crispino,'' Valerian agreed, looking at the unfortunate Alberto, ''although I doubt he is as poisonous. But enough of this sport, diverting as it is. Tell them where they can discover their beloved Bernardo so that we may be on our way. I wish to leave the city at dawn, before these pesky Timoteos of yours can launch yet another sneak attack, as repetition has always held the power to bore me.''

Allegra gave a mighty shrug, clearly not happy to end her sport so soon, and told the men that Bernardo was back at the *pensione*—''sleeping.''

As the pair hastily disappeared down the narrow street, their heavy shoes clanging against the uneven cobblestones, Valerian thanked Tweed for coming to their rescue so promptly and helped Allegra into the closed coach.

"We will return to my hotel, rest for a few hours, *bathe,* and be on our way. Perhaps, signorina, you will amuse me as we travel to Naples by telling me why these Timoteos are after you—and most especially why Bernardo Timoeteo called you his 'love.'"

Allegra burrowed her small body into a dark corner of the coach, her full bottom lip jutting forward in a pout. "Sì, signore, if I must—but I warn you, it is not a pretty story!"

Valerian, his long legs stretched out on the opposite seat, his arms folded negligently across his chest, chuckled deep in his throat. "Somehow, signorina, I think I already suspected as much. Oh, and one more thing, if you please. When we reach my hotel you will enter it from the rear with Tweed—discreetly— then join me upstairs in my rooms."

Allegra sprang forward, her eyes flashing hot sparks in the dark. "*Impossible!* You would treat me like a *prostituta*—a harlot? To sneak into your rooms like some filthy *puttana?* Never! I shall not do it! I should die first!"

Valerian did not move except to slide his gaze to the left to see Allegra throw back her head in an already familiar gesture of defiance. "You're a tiresome enough brat, aren't you?" he offered calmly. "I am not treating you like a prostitute, signorina, even if your manner at the moment would insult one of that ancient profession. If you must know the truth, I do not wish to be seen strolling through a lobby with a barefoot young woman who smells like a sausage. If that is poor-spirited of me, so be it, but I do have some reputation for fastidiousness to uphold. *Comprende?*''

She shrugged expressively yet again, suddenly calm once more. ''It is understood. You are *meticoloso*—a conceited prig.''

Allegra subsided into the corner, her hand going to her bodice, where the remainder of the sausages still resided. ''But I will hate you forever for your terrible insult, signore. Forever!''

CHAPTER TWO

"It all began about six months ago, signore, shortly after my *papà* died."

Valerian sat at his ease on the facing seat of the coach as Allegra began her story. They had spent an uneventful evening at his hotel on the Via del Prato, with Allegra retiring to her rooms without a fuss, her bare feet all but dragging with fatigue.

That was not to say that the morning had been without incident, for she had refused to budge an inch from the hotel without bathing from head to toe in a hip bath she charged Tweed to procure—a sentiment Valerian sincerely seconded—and until she had been served a herculean breakfast of cappuccino, *bisteca alla fiorentina,* and *tortino di carciofi.*

Valerian, accustomed to a lighter breakfast since coming to the Continent, denied himself the opportunity to likewise partake of the thick sliced steak but did sample the eggs with artichokes, a dish whose aroma could not be ignored.

Besides her hygienic and epicurean commands, Allegra harbored only one other demand she wished imparted to Valerian. She had thought long and hard about it during the night, she had told him, and she was not about to travel along the road with him for the days and nights it would take the coach to reach Naples, no matter that no Englishman feels he has seen Italy unless he can claim to have bravely run down the inner slope of the long-dead Mount Vesuvius.

It was out of the question, this constant, unchaperoned togetherness, and so she told him—just as if she hadn't been running about Florence without so much as a *cameriera* in attendance! They were instead to make straight for the coast and the town of Livorno, whence they could hire a small boat to take them to Napoli.

She had even presented Valerian with a crudely drawn map listing a suitable stop along the way where they could sleep (in separate rooms, of course; this part was heavily underlined), change horses, and be assured of a decent meal of Chianti, minestrone, and *funghi alla fiorentina al fuoco di legna*. Allegra's appetite, it was becoming more and more obvious to Valerian, knew no bounds.

Once he had acquiesced to this plan (for any idea that would serve to lessen the amount of time he must spend inside a closed coach with only Allegra for company could only be looked upon as a blessing), they were on their way. Now, an hour later, the coach moving forward at a brisk pace once they had left the city behind them, Allegra finally seemed ready to tell Valerian about the Timoteos.

"Yes," he said, watching as her lower lip began to quiver at the mention of her father. "I learned of his death shortly after I began my quest to locate you. An inflammation of the lungs, I believe?"

Allegra nodded, averting her eyes, then lifted her chin. "It was that terrible Venezia. So beautiful, you know, but so damp. He died in my arms, just as my dearest *madre* breathed her last in his three summers earlier in Modena."

Smiling again, she raised her hands, palms up. "But enough of that! I am the *orfana*—the orphan—but I make my own way. My fame had already begun to spread and my voice was in demand everywhere. I could have been a prima donna—I could still be a prima donna—the best! If only it weren't for that stupid Erberto. Erberto was my manager, you understand." She spread her hands wide, comically rolling her eyes. "Erberto's mouth, signore—*tanto grossa!*"

Valerian chuckled in spite of himself. Allegra was so alive, so mercurial, that he felt constantly on the alert—and continually entertained—by her antics. "And what did Erberto's big mouth do?" he asked as she collapsed against the seat.

She sat forward once more, balancing her elbows on her knees as she spoke so that the lowcut peasant blouse gave him a most pleasant view of her cleavage. Oh, yes, Agnes Kittredge was going to take to her bed for a week once she clapped eyes on her grandniece. "We were in Milano, where I had just had a magnificent triumph at the Teatro alla Scala—"

"You sang at La Scala?" Valerian's tone was openly skeptical.

Allegra tossed back her head, impaling him with her sapphire glare. "No, signore," she shot back. "I swept the stage after the horses were taken off! Of course I sang! Now, if you are done with stupid questions, shall I get on with it?''

Valerian shook his head. "Forgive me, signorina. You must possess a great talent."

She shrugged, then grinned, her natural honesty overcoming her pride. "*Dire una piccola bugia*—it was just a small fib. In truth, I was only one of the chorus—although I did get to die during the finale. It was a very good death—very dramatic, very heart-wrenching. They had no *buffo* that night—no comedy—so I did not get a chance to really show my talent. But, be that as it may, Erberto and I retired to a nearby *caffè* after the performance—for singing always makes me *very* hungry—and that is when it happened."

"Let me hazard a guess. Erberto opened his big mouth."

"*Sì!* It is like this. Erberto is a *fiorentino*, a Florentine, and naturally thinks himself a wag and a wit. But mostly he is a *grullo*, a fool. He is always building himself up by poking fun at someone else. This night his wicked tongue lands on Bernardo Timoteo—something to do with seeing cabbage leaves sticking out of his ears, I think. It is a simple enough jest, hardly what you'd call a triumph of the language, and I am positive it does not linger in stupid Erberto's memory beyond his next bottle of Ruffina."

"But Bernardo takes—I mean, *took* umbrage, and has been chasing the two of you ever since. Now I understand why you were running. But where is this Erberto fellow?"

Allegra leaned forward another six inches, her

hands on her hips. "Who is telling this story, signore, you or I? Take umbrage? No, Bernardo does no such thing, for he is not very smart. Beautiful, yes, but very, very stupid. For myself, I believe it is only sometime later, when one of Milano's good citizens takes the time to explain the insult to Bernardo, that the trouble starts.

"You see, the man probably didn't much like it that an outsider had infringed on what the people of Milano consider theirs—the God-given right to tickle themselves by poking fun at all Timoteos. Oh, yes, signore. I was in the *caffè* long enough that night to hear almost everyone there take a turn at poking fun at *il bello calzolaio*—the beautiful shoemaker."

"Ah," Valerian said ruminatingly, interrupting her yet again. "That would explain the metal mallet, wouldn't it? Oh, I'm sorry, Signorina—please, go on. I'm hanging on your every word, really I am."

Allegra leaned back, making a great business out of crossing her arms beneath her breasts. "No. I don't think so. My English is rusty since my *madre*'s death. You are making fun of me."

Valerian inclined his head slightly, acknowledging her refusal. "Very well, signorina, if that's what you have decided. I shan't beg, you know." So saying, he pushed his curly brimmed beaver down low over his eyes, showing all intentions of taking a nap as Tweed tooled the coach along the narrow, rutted roads.

He had only counted to twenty-seven when Allegra blurted, "Three nights after the incident in the *caffè*—with the help of his brother, Giorgio and his hairy spider cousin Alberto—Bernardo waits in the shadows for Erberto to emerge from the opera house after the performance.''

Her voice lowered dramatically. ''They have, in their ridiculousness, begun the *vendetta*—a hunt for revenge—against my manager! Bernardo taps— boom!—on Erberto's poor skull with that terrible mallet of his even as I watch, helpless.'' She spread her hands, palms upward. ''There is blood every- where!''

''Erberto is dead? I had no idea, signorina,'' he said, pushing up the brim of his hat, the better to see Allegra. Valerian had been reasonably impressed when Bernardo's size (as well as the potential for mayhem provided by the metal mallet the man had carried), but he had not really believed the gorgeous young man capable of murder.

''You poor creature, to have been witness to a mur- der. And they are after you now, to kill you as well in order to cover their tracks. Please, tell me the whole of it.''

She quickly turned her head away, but not before Valerian had seen her smile. ''No, no, signore, I won't go on boring you with my tale of woe. Con- tinue your nap, *per favore*.''

''Little Italian witch,'' Valerian breathed quietly, knowing he had been bested by a mere child, and a female child at that. He sat up straight and offered his apology for teasing her, then begged her to continue with the story of the Timoteos.

''Erberto is not dead—more's the pity. For even Dante's terrible inferno is too good for him,'' she went on, happy to speak now that she was sure she had Fitzhugh's undivided attention. "Once he regained his senses the coward beat a hasty retreat—probably all the way to his uncle's in Sicilia—leaving me alone to starve, for the night of the attack was also the final night of our engagement in Milano. He ran like a rabbit—and took every last bit of my wages with him! I spit on Erberto!"

"Not in *my* coach, you don't!" Valerian cut in firmly, lifting one expressive eyebrow.

She shot him a withering glance. "Of course I won't. Last night I only wished to shock you. You wanted me to be terrible, and I did not wish to be so unkind as to disappoint you. But you would spit on Erberto too, signore, if you knew the whole of it! Bernardo had seen me as I sat in the alley, you understand, holding that thankless Erberto's broken head in my lap—and the fool fell fatally in love with me at that instant!"

"Then Bernardo really is in love with you?"

"Will you never stop asking silly questions and listen? Consider, signore. There I was, still in my stage costume—and a lovely costume it was, all red and glittering gold—sitting in the moonlight...my sapphire eyes awash with tears for the worthless Erberto...my glorious ebony tresses loosed about my shoulders...Erberto's broken head cradled in my lap. I am very beautiful, you know, and I believe Bernardo saw me as a *caritatevole Madonna.*"

"A beneficent madonna? Really?" The child was a complete minx, and Valerian was having a very difficult time keeping his face expressionless as Allegra lifted a hand to push at her hair, striking a dramatic pose. "Don't you think you might be overreacting—not to mention overacting?"

Her right hand sliced the air in a gesture that dismissed Valerian for a fool. "He follows me, does he not—dogging my every footstep these past six months so that I cannot find work, so that I cannot live without looking over my shoulder? He tells Giorgio and Alberto that, with Erberto gone, the *vendetta* is now directed at me, so that all three of them have abandoned the shoemaker shop to make my life a misery. They would not follow him else, you understand.

"But Bernardo has told me—once, when he almost caught me—that he wants only to marry me, to make up for the trouble he caused me by chasing Erberto away. *Stupido!* As if I should spend my life with that empty-headed creature and his beautiful, emptyheaded children! No—I choose to run—to spend my life running, a wild pack of Timoteos forever barking at my heels!"

Valerian reached up a hand to straighten his cravat. "I see now that Duggy's change of heart and imminent demise have come just in time for you, signorina. Considering all that you have told me, I'm surprised it took you so long to accept his offer, for I must admit I too can't believe you have the makings of a dutiful shoemaker's wife."

Rather than become angry, Allegra appeared amused by Valerian's opinion of her worth as a wife for Bernardo. "I should probably take his little metal mallet to his thick skull within a fortnight, signore," she admitted with a grin. "But what is this—we are slowing down!"

She scooted over to the window to see that they were coming into the outskirts of a small town. "Ah, Empoli, and just in time! The inn I directed Tweed to take us to has the most delicious *bruschetta* in the region!"

"*Bruschetta?*" Valerian repeated, scowling. "That's bread drenched in garlic, isn't it?"

"It is nothing so simple. The bread is sliced thick and toasted ever so lightly, then rubbed most generously all over with none but the freshest garlic, olive oil, and salt. I adore it!"

"You will adore it from a distance today, signorina, or else ride up top with Tweed to the next posting inn," Valerian warned her, his expression as stern as his voice. "I am entranced by Italy in general, but I have never learned to share your national love of garlic."

Allegra's chin jutted out as her breast heaved a time or two while she considered this ultimatum. It was raining, and had been raining ever since they had left the hotel. She had been an outside passenger in the wintertime enough to know that she did not wish to be one again. "I will have the minestrone, signore," she said, giving in even though it pained her. "But you will not know what you have missed!"

"Oh, but I already know what I will miss, signorina," he corrected her, reaching for the door as Tweed pulled the coach to a halt. "I will miss an afternoon in peace and quiet while you bear Tweed company—probably the last peace and quiet I shall have until we reach Brighton.''

As Valerian pushed down the coach steps, his back to Allegra, she almost gave in to the urge to lift her foot and push him headfirst through the door and out into the muddy inn yard.

''Ah, signore,'' was all she said a moment later, comically rolling her big blue eyes as Valerian handed her down from the coach, ''you must have a saint on your shoulder. You don't know how lucky, how very lucky, you are!''

Valerian stared after her as she made her way confidently to the inn's entrance, her dark head held high, her step fluidly graceful. The feeling that he was in some sort of unrecognizable danger from this small spitfire of a child was growing ever larger in his chest.

THEY REACHED NAPLES two days later, docking at the bottom of the Via Roma just at sundown, and proceeded directly to the rented villa of Mark Antony Betancourt, Marquess of Coniston, and his wife, Candice. The two were good friends of Valerian's who, upon leaving Rome in October, had instructed him to visit them in their uncle's villa in Naples after the New Year.

His fingers figuratively crossed that the couple would be in residence and not entertaining this evening, Valerian descended from the hastily rented carriage, bidding Allegra to remain behind while he assured himself that the Marquess was at home.

''Will your Marchesa of Coniston bid me to enter through the servants' door as well?'' Allegra asked, reluctant to move. Her stomach and legs had yet to acknowledge that she was back on dry land, because, as she had told Valerian, she didn't have "sailor's feet."

She waited until he had walked away before adding peevishly, "Or do Englishwomen have better manners than Englishmen?"

Valerian, who had already mounted the three shallow stone steps to the front door, turned to smile back at her. "Candie stand on ceremony? I should think not, signorina. I'm sure she'll make us both feel most welcome."

Allegra sniffed and withdrew her head back into the carriage to await developments, as her pride still smarted from having to climb the back stairs at Valerian's hotel in Florence. Her stomach grumbled as she waited for Valerian to summon her and she smiled, knowing that her appetite was returning to normal. With any luck there would be a good Neapolitan cook installed in the villa's kitchen.

Five minutes passed before Valerian opened the door to the carriage and held out his hand for her to descend to the narrow flagway.

"I'm to go to the servants' entrance?" she asked warily.

"The servants' entrance?" exclaimed a female voice from the doorway. "Valerian, what have you been up to with this poor child? I've never before known you to be mean. Cuttingly sarcastic, yes, but never purposely mean. Oh, Tony, Uncle Max—just look at her! She's beautiful! Have you ever seen anything so small as her waist?"

"And I don't think it's her waist we men are looking at, *aingeal cailin,* don't you know," replied a short, rather pudgy man in a curiously lilting baritone. "Reminds me a bit of your sister, Patsy. Isn't that right, m'boyo?"

"I wouldn't know, Max," a third voice supplied, chuckling. "I'm a married man now, you know, and beyond such things."

"Exactly like your sister, Patsy, my love," the Marchioness answered, not sounding in the least upset. "I've always said I would gladly trade her this tiresome hair for her lovely, full bosom."

Allegra, whose gaze had been concentrated on Valerian's face as she tried to take some silent signal from him as to how to go on (a signal which, no matter how hard she looked, never came), lifted her head to confront the three people who had spoken of her as if she weren't really there to listen. Almost instantly her mouth dropped open as she looked at the Marchioness of Coniston, a woman whose ethereal loveliness literally took her breath away.

The Marchioness was tall, and reed-slim, and her beautiful, pale-complexioned, heart-shaped face was animated by a lovely pair of slanted, lively sherry eyes. But it was her hair, a thick mane more white than blonde which fell nearly to her waist, that totally entranced Allegra. Until the Marchioness smiled, that is. Then Allegra was captured and won by the open friendliness in the young woman's expression.

"Come inside, Signorina Crispino, do," the Marchioness commanded, taking Allegra's hand in hers.

"Tony, Uncle Max, come along. Valerian looks as if he could use a tall glass of Chianti."

"What a wonderful idea, Candie. And it's a great thirst I've worked up this day myself, being good," Maximilien P. Murphy answered brightly as the five of them headed inside, passing by a small group of interested servants.

Valerian slipped his arm around the older man's shoulders as they walked across the marble foyer and into the main *salotto*. "It's strange that you should mention being good, Max," he said companionably, "for I've been wondering—how would you like to be *bad* for a while? Nothing terrible, you understand, just perhaps a momentary resurrection of the Conte di Casals, the Italian Count Tony told me you played to perfection in London. Would you impersonate him again—just long enough for the Conte to procure a passport for Signorina Crispino here?"

"That's it? One tiny passport?" Maximilien answered, frowning. "That's no harder than tripping off a log. Done and done, my boyo!"

"Valerian! Shame on you. And shame on you, Tony, my love, for telling tales out of school!" the Marchioness, overhearing, accused. "Uncle Max doesn't do that sort of thing anymore, Valerian. You know that. After all, now that Tony and I have our sweet little Murphy, we want our son to get to know his uncle as a free man—and not just as a poor wretch we take oranges to at the local *prigione*."

Allegra, who had been led to a chair by the Marquess, looked up at Lady Coniston in confusion. "Prison! Your uncle is a criminal?" she asked, biting her lip at the insult. "*Scusi!* I mean to say—" She turned to Valerian, who was now holding a wineglass and looking very much at home and at his ease. "Well, don't just stand there! Help me, Fitzhugh, *per favore!* What did I mean to say?"

Lady Coniston promptly sat down beside Allegra and patted her hand. "Don't apologize, my dear, for it was an honest mistake. You see, dearest Uncle Max and I traveled about the world for many years before Tony and I married, and we—well, you might say we indulged in a wee bit of stage-playing from time to time when the need arose."

"Is that right? And 'tis that what you call it now, me fine *Marchioness?* We lived higher than O'Hara's hog on that 'stage-playing,' if memory serves," Maximilien retorted, his round face turning a violent red, although Allegra, watching him, was very sure he was not really angry, but was only indulging in a little more stage-acting of his own. They were an unusual group, she acknowledged silently, but there was a lot of love in this villa, and she felt a momentary pang at the remembered loss of her own family.

"High as O'Hara's hog, is it? And twice as much time was spent lower than O'Malley's well, *Uncail.* I remember that as well," Lady Coniston shot back, not without humor. "Now, do we waste time splitting hairs, or do we help Valerian and Signorina Crispino with their little problem? Uncle Max, your Conte di Casals may get the passport, but I don't wish to hear how. I'm a mother now—and, like my husband, 'past such things.'"

"It's turning into an Irish shrew ye are, darlin'," Max groused before downing a glass of wine.

"Valerian," she went on, unheeding, still holding Allegra's hand as she turned to her other guest, "all we heard when Tony and I last saw you in Rome was that you were off to find Lord Dugdale's long-lost granddaughter and transport her to Brighton. I see the granddaughter before me, and I congratulate you on your success, but I sense that more is involved in this story. Please, if I promise to have the servants lay out some refreshments in the *sala da pranzo,* you must tell us everything, from the very beginning!"

Allegra's ears pricked up at the mention of food, her recent seasickness forgotten, and she squeezed Lady Coniston's hands appreciatively. "I will tell you everything, dear Marchesa, I promise, all about my singing, my life, and even the terrible Timoteos— directly *after* we have eaten!"

A FULL TWO WEEKS passed in relative bliss for Allegra, for in the Marchioness of Coniston she had found her first true female friend since childhood. Lady Coniston, or Candie, as she had begged Allegra to address her, was more than gracious, more than interested—she was a true sister of the heart.

For Candie had not always led a life of comfort; she had known poverty, she had known fear, and she had learned to make her own way, by whatever means she could. But, like Allegra, she had never sacrificed her honor in order to fill her belly.

Candie had been rewarded for her purity with the love of Tony Betancourt, a man Allegra found to be immensely wonderful, and with the birth of their son, Murphy, an adorable blond cherub of two years who held his uncle Max's heart in his chubby little hands.

Could there be such a similarly rosy future in Brighton for someone like Allegra? Somehow, she doubted it, no matter how enthusiastic Candie was about her prospects.

To that end, and over Allegra's protests, Candie had set out to provide her young guest with a complete new wardrobe the very morning after Valerian and Allegra's arrival in Naples. Although Italian styles were still woefully behind those of Paris, there existed enough modistes sufficiently schooled in the art of copying for Allegra to acquire a fairly extensive wardrobe that would be considered not only acceptable but wonderfully stylish by the ladies of Brighton.

But the Marchioness was not content to merely dress her young guest in fine feathers. Oh, no. She spent long hours schooling Allegra in proper deportment (including at least one stern lecture concerning Allegra's tendency to gesture with her hands as she spoke, an entirely too Italian habit), and had helped her to weed most Italian words and phrasing from her vocabulary, permitting her to use only those considered suitably Continental and sure to impress her English relatives.

"I was the Conte di Casals's niece Gina more than once in the past, you understand," the Marchioness had informed her as the two sat alone late one night over Allegra's lessons, "so I have a fairly good notion as to how you should go on. Have I told you about the time—I was just a young girl, I believe—

that Uncle Max wrangled us an audience with the Pope?''

''His Holiness!'' Allegra had exclaimed, much impressed. ''I once sang a solo for the Bishop of Bologna, but it is not the same, is it?''

Yes, there were many lessons, but there were just as many stories, and just as many shared reminiscences between the new friends, quite a few of them having to do with the at-times-almost-bizarre courtship of Candice Murphy by Mark Antony Betancourt, Seventh Marquess of Coniston. The Marquess, it seemed, had until his marriage been known all over London as Mister Overnite: a carefree, heartbreakingly handsome man who supposedly had held the modern-day British record for dallying the whole night long in more society matrons' beds than half the husbands in the Upper Ten Thousand.

It hadn't been easy for Tony to understand that his bachelor days were effectively over from the first moment he'd clapped eyes on the mischievous Miss Murphy, but—as Candie, blushing, told Allegra—he had lived to give proof to the adage that reformed rakes make the *very* best of husbands.

As for Allegra's singing career, it had been left to Valerian to explain to her that this, alas, was over, finally and completely. It was not to be mentioned in company, it was not to be considered as a viable part of her future—it simply was not to be thought of, ever again!

Only the quick-witted Tony had been able to save Valerian from Allegra's employment of a particularly vile Italian curse, which he did by quickly pointing out that there was nothing wrong with Allegra considering herself a talented amateur.

"Why, as a matter of fact," he had interjected cleverly, winking at his appreciative wife, "Prinny himself is quite a devotee of Italian opera. You're bound to be the sensation of the age, Allegra, once you sing for him, for many of his guests perform at the Marine Pavilion after one of his Highness's hours-long dinner parties."

"Yes, the dinner parties," Valerian had added, knowing by now where to aim his darts where Allegra was concerned. "I heard it said that there are often two dozen main dishes served in one evening," he slid in, watching as Allegra's sapphire eyes opened wide. "That's not to mention the many side dishes, cakes, puddings, pastries, and the rest. Although I have not yet had the pleasure, Duggy is one of Old Swellfoot's cronies, signorina, so you are sure to be invited, if you can just learn to behave yourself."

All in all, Allegra had become not only resigned to leaving Italy but anxious to reach England and her mother's birthplace, although it was with tears in her eyes that she waved good-bye to the Betancourts as the ship pulled away from the pier, her newly obtained passport safely in Valerian's possession.

Then, suddenly, all her new finery to one side and her more refined English forgotten, she pointed to the dock, hopping on one slippered foot as she exclaimed, "*Impossible!* It is that terrible Bernardo—here, in Napoli! How has he found me? Again he shows up unwanted, *come un cane nella chiesa*— like a dog in a church!"

As Bernardo ran to the very edge of the pier, tears streaming down his handsome face and looking for all the world as if he was about to throw himself into the water in order to swim out to the ship, Allegra struck her right arm straight out in front of her, tucked her middle two fingers beneath her thumb, and shouted dramatically, *"Si rompe il corno!"*

Immediately Bernardo stepped back as if stunned, clutching his chest.

"You're going to break his horns?" Valerian asked from beside her, watching bemusedly as her small but voluptuous figure was shown to advantage by her antics. "Why don't I believe that is some sort of quaint Italian farewell?"

Allegra threw back her head, her long black hair blowing in the wind, since she had shunned Candie's suggestion that she wear one of the new bonnets Valerian's money had bought her. "I wished evil on him, signore. Great evil such as only another Italian can imagine!"

"Oh, you did, did you? And now you will kindly take it off again," Valerian commanded, shaking his head. "Otherwise the lovesick fool will be on my conscience forevermore. You're leaving Italy, signorina, so you can afford to be magnanimous. Bernardo Timoteo and his cohorts can no longer harm you."

Allegra turned to Valerian, her face alight with glee. *"Magnifico,* signore! You are right! I, Allegra Crispino, will be magnanimous!" She leaned over the railing, waving a white handkerchief at the openly sobbing Bernardo. *"Addio, caro Bernardo addio!"*

she called brightly, until the handsome young man on the pier heard her and began waving in return.

Valerian, well pleased with himself, smiled and waved to Bernardo as well, hardly believing he was actually on his way to Brighton at last, to achieve the long-awaited removal of the mercurial Allegra Crispino from his guardianship.

An odd, unrecognizable sensation in his stomach at the thought of depositing Allegra with Lord Dugdale and then walking away prompted him to turn his head and look down at the strange young girl.

"Allegra!" he was startled into saying, for she was gripping the rail with both hands, huge, crystalline tears running down her wind-reddened cheeks. "Why are you crying? Surely you're not going to miss having the Timoteo dogs barking at your heels?"

"I shall never see my beloved Italia again, Valerian," she answered in a small voice, her gaze still intent on the rapidly disappearing shoreline as she gave out with a shuddering sigh. "My *madre,* my *papà* they live in that earth. They are lost to me forever; all of what is home to me is now gone, while I sail away to an uncertain future with a grandfather I don't know. I didn't know how much it would hurt, Valerian, or how very much frightened I would feel."

Before he could think, before he could weigh the right or the wrong of it, Valerian gathered Allegra's small frame close against his chest, where she remained, her arms wrapped tightly around his waist, as, together, they watched the only homeland she had ever known fade from sight.

CHAPTER THREE

AGNES KITTREDGE sat in the outdated drawing room she would most happily have given her best Kashmir shawl to redecorate, awaiting the arrival of her children, seventeen-year-old Isobel and her older brother, Gideon, who had reached the age of three and twenty, Agnes was sure, thanks only to his fond mama's most assiduous nursing of his delicate constitution.

Mrs. Kittredge's brother, Baron Dennis Dugdale, was upstairs in his rooms, his gouty right foot swathed in bandages Agnes would much rather see bound tightly about his clearly disordered head.

She was furious, Agnes Kittredge was, pushed nearly to the brink of distraction by the disquieting thought that her beloved brother, Dennis, could have the nerve to recover his health after he had most solemnly promised that his demise was imminent. Was there no one, who could be trusted to keep his word anymore, not even a brother?

Not only had her aging sibling once more become the possessor of depressingly good health, but his general demeanor had reverted to one of such high good humor that Agnes, who had never been a tremendous advocate of levity, was lately finding herself hard-pressed to keep a civil tongue in her head whenever the jolly Baron was about.

Lord Dugdale's near-constant, jocular remarks alluding to a ''change in the wind,'' and his oblique hints at a coming ''surprise to knock your nose more sideways than it already is, Aggie,'' were not only most depressingly annoying, they were beginning to worry her very much.

Everything had always been so settled, so regulated, in the life they all lived at Number 23 in the Royal Crescent Terrace. Agnes ruled, Isobel preened, Gideon gambled, and dearest Denny paid the bills. It was all so simple, so orderly. Now Lord Dugdale was making noises as if this arrangement no longer could be regarded as the ordinary, and that soon there would come a major readjustment in all their lives.

Agnes had agreed with this notion in part at first, when the Baron had spoken so earnestly of his imminent demise. There most assuredly would be changes at Number 23 when that unhappy day finally dawned.

Agnes would still rule, Isobel would still preen, Gideon would still gamble. But forever gone from the scene would be Lord Dugdale and his annoying habit of closely questioning the amount of the bills his family presented to him with every expectation that they be paid at once, and without his first issuing a sermon about the evils of incautious spending.

Once her brother, rest his soul, was safely underground, Agnes would be free to run the household exactly as she wished, without the wearying necessity to beg for every groat. This sort of ''change'' Agnes had looked forward to with great expectation, nearly unmixed with sorrow for the soon-to-be-departed brother, who, after all, had led a good long life and deserved his rest.

It was all that new doctor's fault, Agnes had decided when her brother, far from sliding conveniently into his grave, began to make a near-miraculous recovery from a violent uproar of the bowels. Who ever heard of such a thing? No bleeding. No leeches. No thin gruel. Just plenty of fresh air, exercise, and good, hearty food. The treatment should have killed the Baron, but it hadn't.

Agnes hadn't allowed the doctor back in the house since the first day Lord Dugdale had sat up and loudly called for his pipe and a full bottle of his favorite cherry ripe.

"Not that it did me a penny worth of good," she groused, arranging her shawl more firmly about her bony shoulders as she thought of her brother's refusal to suffer an immediate relapse. "The man's body has been restored at the cost of his wits. It had been nearly three months, and still we must hear daily about this surprise of his. It is time and more I consider placing the poor, sainted man in an institution where there are those trained in dealing with delusional lunatics such as Denny."

"Talking to yourself, Mama? I must admit I do know of some who do so from time to time, but then I believe those people are usually rather deep in their cups. Have you been nipping while my back was turned, Mama? It isn't like you; but then this entire household has been rather irregular for weeks on end now, hasn't it?''

Agnes Kittredge looked up at the sound of her beloved Gideon's voice. "Darling!" she exclaimed, patting the space beside her on the settee. "Come sit down and tell me how you feel this morning. You were abroad quite late last night, I believe. The damp night air isn't good for you, you know. Have you breakfasted? I expressly ordered the eggs be poached this morning, as they are much more suited to your delicate constitution in that form than the hard-cooked variety you persist in eating whenever my back is turned.''

He sat down dutifully, spreading his coattails neatly as he did so. "I shunned eggs entirely this morning, Mama, in favor of dry toast dipped in watered wine, for I woke with the most shocking headache. Do you think it's coming on to rain? It couldn't have been the canary I partook of last night, for you know I never drink to excess.''

"Indeed no, Gideon. You would never do that, not with your fragile system." Agnes turned to look adoringly upon her son. Gideon Kittredge was as handsome as his mother and sister were plain—although how this quirk of nature came about no one save Lord Dugdale, who once mentioned the idea of his sister having played her husband false at least the once, had ever been able to understand the phenomenon.

Gideon had been born scarcely five months after his parents' marriage, a sickly babe whose small size and poor chances for survival lent at least partial credence to the outrageous fib that he had been born

much too soon due to an unfortunate fright his mother
had taken at the sight of a tumbling dwarf in the small
traveling circus she and her husband had chanced
upon the same day Agnes was delivered of her first-
born child.

When Gideon didn't expire as expected, Agnes,
through guilt over her lie or natural motherly devotion
only she knew, threw her entire energies into coddling
and protecting the child well past the point of necessity or even common sense.

Gideon's sniffles were a sure sign of a lung inflammation, his cough no less than threatening consump-
tion, his sighs a dire portent of some crippling, dis-
abling condition that must be averted at all costs.
Isobel was conceived and born almost without Agnes's notice and shuffled off to a separate nursery so
that she could not contaminate her brother's air.

When Mister Kittredge had the misfortune to break
his neck in a hunting accident, Agnes had little time
for grieving, for she was too busy thanking her lucky
stars that the man hadn't instead decided to succumb
to some lingering illness that might either be passed
on to Gideon or take her away overlong from her
main project in life, that of taking care of her son.

That Gideon had grown from a whining, totally un-
lovable child into a self-indulgent adult concerned
only with his own wants and desires could not be
surprising. Even less of a revelation was that he thoroughly disliked his mother, the woman having earned
his disgust because of his easy ability to manipulate
her.

Moving closer to her now, Gideon laid his dark

head on Agnes's shoulder and gazed up into her watery blue eyes. "You appear distressed, dearest Mama. Is there anything I can do to help? I promise I shall not let this crushing headache stay me from performing whatever deed you should ask of me. After all, I owe my life to you, as well I know."

Agnes blinked twice, masterfully holding back loving tears. "I shouldn't think to bother your aching head, my darling," she declared passionately, daring to touch a hand to his smooth cheek. "It's just your uncle Denny again. I fear he is becoming worse with each passing day."

Gideon turned his head slightly and stifled a yawn. "Really? In what way?"

"Why, this morning he is insisting on coming downstairs, even though his foot is still wrapped up like some heathen mummy, and his valet has told me your uncle actually intends to see his tailor this afternoon to order an entire new suit of clothes. Now why would he need new clothes? It isn't as if he doesn't have a closet full of them."

"All displaying his love of food, for the dear man seems to find it necessary to wear what he eats," Gideon supplied helpfully.

"Precisely so, my dear," Agnes concurred feelingly. "I should think he'd be more concerned with the fact that you have been seen in the same evening dress at least three times this year. If anyone is in dire need of a new wardrobe, dearest, it is you, who shows his tailor to such advantage."

There was a slight movement at the doorway, followed by a decidedly unladylike snort from Miss Isobel Kittredge, who had just entered the room.

"Toadeating Mama again, Gideon?" the young lady asked, taking up a seat across from the settee. "I'm surprised you haven't hopped into her lap to ask her to tell you a story. Or would you rather tell her a story, possibly the one about your latest venture into the land of the sharpers?"

Agnes wrinkled her forehead, at least as much as the tightly done-up bun perched atop her head allowed her to do. "Sharpers? What are sharpers, Gideon? I don't believe I've ever heard the term."

Gideon, sitting up smartly once more, shot his sister a fulminating look. "Pernicious little brat," he gritted from between his even white teeth as Isobel, obviously well pleased with herself, made a great business out of straightening a lace doily on the table beside her.

"Pernicious, am I?" she countered, lifting hazel eyes as depressingly watery as her mother's to her brother's face. "Since you have roused the energy necessary to be insulting, I can only imagine that I am right and you are scorched again."

"Gideon?" Agnes prompted, fighting the feeling that yet another score of gray hairs were about to sprout overnight on her already nearly white head. "Is your sister correct? Have you been gambling again?"

Sparing a moment to send his sister another fulminating, I'll-see-to-you-later look, Gideon picked up his mother's left hand and held it firmly between both of his. "I must admit to a shocking run of bad luck, Mama, but it is nothing to fret about, I promise. The devil was in it last night, that's all, but I'll come about as soon as you can get Uncle Denny to advance you a small pittance on the household allowance.''

Agnes's thin face took on a pinched expression. "How much, Gideon? I cannot fob your uncle off with another story about the price of candles. He has his wits about him again, you know, at least in the area of his finances. Tell me quickly, before I conjure up some horrendous sum.''

"A mere monkey, Mama," Gideon mumbled into his cravat. "Five hundred pounds. Four hundred, actually, but I also placed a small wager with a certain party about the outcome of a race. Dratted horse stumbled going round the turn."

"Five hundred pounds! I will never be able to extract so much from your uncle as that!''

"Of course you will, Mama—for me.'' He brought his mother's hand to his mouth, firmly pressing his lips against the papery skin. "And I promise, Mama, I shall eschew racing from this moment on. I don't know how I got involved in such a harebrained thing, for you know I can't abide horses. It was all George Watson's idea—he goaded me into the wager when my spirits were at a low ebb!''

"Of course he did," Agnes agreed immediately, pressing her cheek against her son's hands. "I never did like that George—and his grandfather smells entirely too much of the shop to suit me, as I recall. You would be wise to eschew George in the future as well, my darling.''

"George tied him up and forced him to make a wager against his will," Isobel spat mockingly, shaking her head. "Honestly, Mama, he takes you in like a green goose, over and over again. Gideon is a dedicated gamester. When are you going to get that fact into your head? Why, he probably has a wager with George right now on how long it will take you to come up with the blunt to settle his latest debt."

"Isobel!" Agnes exclaimed, stung. "You will apologize at once! I vow, your overweening jealousy of your brother makes me wonder if I have nurtured a viper at my bosom."

Gideon took that moment to cough delicately into his fist.

"Now look what you've done!" Agnes exclaimed, immediately pressing a hand to her son's forehead to check for fever. "You've brought on one of Gideon's spasms. Such an unnatural child!"

"It wasn't—*a-ahumph, a-ahumph*—my dearest sister's viperish tongue—*a-aumph*—that upset me, Mama," Gideon corrected quickly, his strong voice giving the lie to his continuing bout of coughing. "It is the money that worries me. George can be so demanding—and it is, after all, a debt of honor. If only I should be assured that Uncle Denny won't cut up stiff—"

"No, no, of course he won't. I shan't even mention your name," Agnes assured her son even as she shot her smirking daughter a quelling look. "I shall approach your uncle this afternoon."

"Without fail?" Gideon asked, somehow managing to produce a slight sheen of feverish perspiration on his smooth upper lip.

"Without fail, my darling," Agnes vowed, then

gave a quick silencing wave of her hand as she heard her brother's limping gait approaching outside in the hallway.

"La, yes," she exclaimed quickly in an overly hearty voice that was sure to carry as far as the foyer. "I have just come from prayers in my room, yet again thanking the good Lord on my knees for your uncle's miraculous recovery. I should think the fine air of Brighton has had much to do with his renewed good health, but the good Lord must be thanked for that good air as well, mustn't He, children?"

"Spouting gibberish again, Aggie?" Lord Dugdale asked from the doorway, where he stood leaning heavily on the bulbous head of his cane. "If you wish to thank anyone, thank Valerian Fitzhugh—for it's he who saved me, sure as check. Great faith I have in that boy, and it's sure to be rewarded any day now with the most wonderful surprise a man could push himself up from the brink of the grave to accept."

He took two more steps into the room before Isobel rose to take his arm, helping him to the chair she had just vacated. "You mustn't push yourself, Uncle, not on your first day downstairs. There you go," she complimented as the Baron lowered himself heavily into the chair. "Now if you'll just let me place this footstool here for you to rest that leg on—there! Mama, Gideon—doesn't Uncle Denny look much more the thing?"

Lord Dugdale looked from sister to niece to nephew, his squat, heavy body all but wedged into the chair as he presented himself for their scrutiny. What his relatives saw, other than the truly magnificent cocoon of snowy white bandages stuck to the lower half of his right leg and foot, was a no-longer-young man with a sparse, partial circlet of gray hair banding his head directly above his ears, leaving his shiny bald pate to cast a glare in the afternoon sunlight coming through a nearby window.

His eyes, the same watery blue of his sister's but with a multitude of cunning if not intelligence lurking in their depths, returned their piercing looks, yet his round-as-a-pie plate face was carefully expressionless. Yes, it was the same old Baron Dugdale they had known forever—complete to the food stains on his loosely tied cravat and too-tight waistcoat.

"Well, this is something new, Uncle Denny," Isobel piped up at last, perching her thin frame on a corner of the footstool as she looked up at the Baron. "You've been hinting about this surprise for weeks, but I've never heard Mister Fitzhugh's name mentioned before this moment. Why, it must be three years or more since he's been home to Brighton. Ever since Waterloo, I imagine. Is that the surprise? That Valerian—I mean, Mister Fitzhugh—is returning home?"

Gideon rose to stand behind the settee. "Don't drool, Isobel; it doesn't become you. Why, you were scarcely out of swaddling clothes when Valerian Fitzhugh took off for the Continent. Don't tell me you still fancy yourself in love with the man. Lord, that's pathetic!"

Isobel's normally sallow complexion visibly paled and a small white line tightened about her thin lips. "Gideon Kittredge—you take that back!" she gritted, pointing a shaking finger in his direction. "Mama! Make him take that back!"

"I won't take it back," Gideon declared, moving to stand more directly behind his mother. "You've been embroidering slippers with his name on them every Christmas in the hope he'll come back from the Continent and sweep you off your feet and into his waiting arms. Well, let me tell you, sister mine, those slippers will grow whiskers before Valerian Fitzhugh tosses more than a crust of bread in your direction!"

"Children—children! Stop this at once!" Agnes pleaded, sure that Gideon would soon overheat himself with his exertion. "Isobel, remember your brother's frail constitution."

"Odds bobs, woman," Lord Dugdale chortled. "The little bugger has the constitution of a horse, if only you'd scrape the scales of mother love from your eyes long enough to see it. Now, does anyone wish to hear about my surprise or not? With Valerian's letter reaching me the very day I turned my head away from death's dark door, I figure the time is about right for my little announcement. Any later and it will most probably be too late."

"I fear, dear Baron, you have already left it too late, if I have guessed correctly and you have failed to acquaint your family with the purpose of my mission," pronounced a smoothly articulate voice from the doorway to the hall. "Pardon me for having bypassed your butler and choosing to announce myself, but after all this time I could barely contain my anxiety to present you with my traveling companion."

"Valerian!" Isobel all but screamed, hopping up

from the footstool to raise a trembling hand to her nonexistent breast. "Mama, Gideon—look! It is Valerian!"

Fitzhugh walked fully into the room to make his bows to the company. "Such a rousing welcome, Miss Kittredge," he said, inclining his head over her outstretched paw. "I vow I would have returned to Brighton much earlier had I known I would be accorded such a heartwarming greeting. I left you a child, but I have returned to see the woman."

He turned to the Baron. "Having seen no crepe hatchment on the knocker, I had already assumed you still lingered, awaiting my return, but now I see that you have made a full recovery. This knowledge makes my time spent fulfilling your request even more personally rewarding, as I have a sentimental heart and shall greatly enjoy this coming family reunion."

Baron Dugdale snorted once, pushing himself about in the chair so as to get a look at the now vacant doorway. "Never mind all that sweet talk, man— where is she? You wrote from Florence, promising to have her here within three months. What did you do—leave her at the dock to guard the luggage? Must I fetch her the rest of the way myself?"

"Her?" Agnes directed a long, dispassionate stare at her brother until at last, her eyes narrowing even as twin flags of color began waving brightly in her thin cheeks, she declared tightly, "Dennis Dugdale— you *didn't!* You *couldn't!* You *wouldn't! How dare you?* I won't have that foreign baggage in my house!"

With Agnes's words the drawing room was immediately transformed into a hotbed of mingled questions and accusations, all delivered in full voice and with the sharp rapidity of gunshots.

"Your house? *Your house!* I could be three days dead and it would still be my house, woman. It will always be my house!"

"Who did Valerian bring from Florence, Mama? Do you know her? Is it some relative of Aunt Mary's husband? But I thought Uncle Denny disowned Aunt Mary years ago, and Aunt Mary's dead, isn't she?"

"A foreign woman? I knew you were off to France and such. So you've been in Italy as well, have you, you lucky dog? Tell me, are Italian women as hot-blooded as I've heard, old man? Does she sing? I hear they all warble like little songbirds. What's Uncle going to do with her—give her to Prinny?"

"My hartshorn! Where is my hartshorn? Quickly, Gideon—my hartshorn. I shall perish in a fit, I just know it!"

"I'll give you a fit, you daft female! Odds bobs, but I don't know why I've put up with you all these long years!"

"Rompere le uova nel paniere di qualcuno."

Immediately there came a crashing silence throughout the drawing room as all the voices cut off abruptly and all heads turned to locate the person who had uttered the foreign gibberish.

Valerian turned as well, to see that Allegra had entered the room, still clad in her traveling cloak, to stand slightly behind him, her hand barely touching his arm. "Yes, indeed, Signorina Crispino," he agreed quietly, "it certainly would appear as if we have well and truly broken the eggs in someone's basket. In *all* their baskets, as a matter of fact, save your grandfather's. He is that gentleman seated over there—the gentleman wearing that extremely wide smile."

Valerian turned back to the occupants of the room, bowing once more. "Mrs. Agnes Kittredge, Miss Isobel Kittredge—Gideon. Allow me to present to you Signorina Allegra Crispino, daughter of the late Mary Dugdale Crispino and only granddaughter of Baron Dennis Dugdale. Signorina Crispino—your loving, devoted family."

"Come state?" Allegra asked, her chin high as she dared anyone to say a single word more. *"Grazie per la cordiale accoglienza!"*

Valerian looked down at Allegra curiously, wondering why the young woman had chosen to speak in Italian after all of his and Candie's warnings to the contrary, but he decided to go along with her for the moment, for he was sure she was justifiably nervous at this first meeting.

"Signorina Crispino asks how you all are and thanks you for your most *cordial* welcome. Italians, you may infer from her words, are not unconversant with sarcasm," he added quietly as her fingertips dug into his forearm.

"We've had a most arduous journey here from Naples, what with storms at sea and Signorina Crispino's lack of what she delightfully terms 'sailor's feet,' but we are here now, having dispensed with the signorina's temporary chaperon at the dock a scant hour ago. Her baggage will be delivered directly, at which time I am sure she will wish to retire to her rooms for a rest. In the meantime, I am assured you, Mrs. Kittredge, will endeavor to make your niece as comfortable as possible.''

''But of course!'' Agnes exclaimed quickly, seeing the warning in her brother's eyes and not daring any further revolt—at least not at this moment. ''We must make dear Mary's child welcome! Unfortunately, we have no room ready—thanks to my dear brother's misguided love of surprises—but we shall just have to make do, won't we, Isobel? How long will the dear child be staying in our country? This is just a visit—isn't it?''

Allegra's slightly husky voice was low and laden with disdain. *''Tu hai il cuore di un coniglio.''*

Valerian's lips quivered appreciatively as Allegra's quick remark threatened to unleash a bark of laughter that could only serve to shatter the already tense atmosphere in the room into a million jagged pieces.

But Allegra had taken one look and seen straight through the woman to her self-serving core. Indeed, as Allegra had said, Agnes Kittredge possessed the heart of a rabbit. The woman might detest the thought of being kind to Allegra with every fiber of her being, but she wasn't about to jeopardize her own position in the household by standing on her principles in front of her clearly determined brother.

''Signorina Crispino says for me to tell you that you are very kind, Mrs. Kittredge,'' Valerian said at last, when the prolonged silence had become almost unbearable, Allegra's ever-tightening grip on his forearm threatening to shut off his blood supply to that necessary limb.

"Yes, yes, enough of that, boy," the Baron interrupted testily. "This is demmed awkward, but I can't get up just anytime I want. This miserable foot, you understand. Bring the gel round here so I can get a good look at her. I never thought I'd live to see the day my Mary's child would be here with me. I did her mother a terrible wrong, you know, cutting her off without a farthing when she ran off with that Italian bastard—but it's time and more I made amends.

"Ah, there she is," he said, sighing, as Valerian all but pushed Allegra forward so that she stood in front of the footstool. "Take off her cloak, for pity's sake, so I can really see her. Little thing, ain't she—all eyes and hair."

Allegra's small hands balled into fists at her sides and she glared up at Valerian accusingly. Leaning down close to her ear as he helped her off with her cloak, he whispered in Italian, "It isn't my fault the old boy's still alive. Besides, I think you'll fare better this way than if you had to deal directly with your aunt. She'd make the Timoteos look like a stroll in the park, to my way of thinking."

A moment later Allegra was divested of her cloak, to stand before her grandfather in the modishly styled morning gown of green-and-white sprigged muslin Candie had deemed demure enough, yet sufficiently sophisticated, to give a good first impression.

Lord Dugdale rubbed his hands together in glee as his watery blue eyes made a careful assessment of his granddaughter. "Oh, this is more than I could have hoped for, Valerian, truly it is. Why, she'll have half the bucks in Brighton drooling all over her slippers! She doesn't much favor my Mary, except perhaps a little around the chin—it's Mary's stubborn chin to the life—but I don't see any of the father in her either, thank God. Yes, with her looks and figure—and the plum I plan to give her—she'll do just fine!''

''A plum! Never say you're going to give her a plum!''

This outburst came from Gideon, who had been remarkably quiet up to this point as he had been very preoccupied in cudgeling his brain to find some way of bringing the conversation around to his crushing need for five hundred pounds before nightfall. However, the mention of a dowry of one hundred thousand pounds had served to bring him unhesitatingly to attention. ''Why don't you give her the house and all the rest while you're at it?'' he asked facetiously.

''I plan to, nephew,'' Lord Dugdale responded swiftly, still looking at Allegra. ''But not quite yet. I've more than made up my mind to stay aboveground a while longer, just so that I can see my granddaughter comfortably settled.''

''The—the house? *This* house? And all your fortune? Denny—what about me? What about Gideon—my children?''

Lord Dugdale reached out to take hold of Allegra's hands, smiling up into his granddaughter's stony face. ''What about 'em, Agnes? You'll all have your allowances as usual and a roof over your heads. But that's all I can give you. I had a vision, you see, whilst I lay dying. An angel came to me and asked how I thought I could face Saint Peter at the Golden Gates, knowing what terrible sin I had committed against my only child.''

He sat forward, not without great effort, and looked around Allegra to his sister. ''I'll feed you and yours, Agnes, and I'll house and clothe you, but you must understand. I'll be damned for a bloody fool if I'll burn in Hell for you!''

Allegra tugged at Valerian's sleeve so that he bent down to hear her whisper in Italian, ''I've heard enough for now. I think it would be a very good time for me to drop into a most graceful, affecting swoon, don't you? Please catch me, *per favore,* for I shouldn't wish to fall on *Nonno*'s poor foot.''

Before Valerian could protest, Allegra raised a hand to her temple, moaned once—a truly wonderful, anguished, theatrical moan—as her huge sapphire eyes fluttered closed behind a thick veil of long, sweeping black lashes.

A moment later, and much against his inclination, Valerian found himself cradling her small, limp body against his chest.

CHAPTER FOUR

VALERIAN STOOD outside the small bedchamber into which he had ten minutes previously deposited the limp yet curiously clinging body of Allegra Crispino, still wondering how he, a normally well-regulated, rational man of no mean intelligence, had come to be in his current insane position.

Much as he had been simultaneously attracted to and repelled by Allegra during the time they had spent together in Italy, he had more than once rejoiced in her inability to leave her cabin after their ship had put to sea. This lengthy respite from her volatile presence, which had lasted for the entirety of their journey to Brighton, had almost totally cured him of his curious attraction for the imp—or so he'd thought, until the moment she had "fainted" into his arms.

He'd had every intention—every serious, well-thought-out intention—of depositing Allegra with her English relatives within an hour of docking and then retiring to the comfort (and personal safety) of his own estate just outside the seaside town for a well-deserved rest.

He knew now, however—intentions being what they were, and Allegra being who she was—that the "thought" never really had much chance of being transformed into "deed." Besides, if nothing else, he could console himself with the notion that he was just too curious to leave.

He should have realized Allegra was up to something the moment the little minx had opened her mouth downstairs and spoken in Italian, rather than the English he and Candie had warned her would be a major asset in having her accepted by her mother's family.

But why should he have been taken off guard? Allegra's actions since entering the Baron's residence, Valerian thought now—considering the day he'd already had—should not have surprised him in the least. They should only have made him wonder if there existed any limit to Allegra's capacity for outrageous unpredictability.

He once more considered the fact that she'd had the audacity to emerge from her stateroom this morning looking as fresh and as lovely as only a naturally beautiful woman could appear. If she really had been ill for the length of the journey, as her hastily employed English chaperon had most earnestly informed him she was, the ravages of mal de mer certainly hadn't shown either in her face or on her still petitely voluptuous figure.

Her adorably vibrant face; her soft, yielding figure. Valerian shook his head, banishing such dangerous thoughts, and brought himself back to the matter at hand.

She had cried illness, yet she appeared even more healthy now than she had after a week of rest and indulgence in Naples. He had very much wanted to question her about this seeming inconsistency, but Allegra had kept him so busy answering her rapid-fire questions about Brighton as the carriage had rumbled through the streets that there hadn't been time.

No. He had to be honest with himself. He hadn't wanted to ask her how she'd managed to banish her supposed seasickness so quickly. What he had really wanted to know, still longed to know, was why she had felt the need to take such pains to elude his company while they had been aboard ship. Was he truly that repulsive to her?

If only they'd had more time to talk. If only her arrival hadn't thrown the entire household into such turmoil, thanks mostly, Valerian had decided, to both Baron Dugdale's refusal to expire as promised and his decision to keep his granddaughter's advent into the Dugdale household a secret.

He had been embarrassed for the lot of them, Valerian had, but he could not in all honesty say that he had expected less from the Kittredges or the Baron, none of whom were known for either their tact or their reticence.

Valerian pulled out his pocket watch and marked the time, suddenly once more anxious to be on his way. He should have quit the house the moment he had safely deposited Allegra on the bed. That's what any sane man—even a very curious sane man—would have done. Perhaps he could convince himself it had only been Allegra's swift delivery of a discreet yet painful warning pinch to his ribs when he had voiced to Agnes Kittredge his intention to depart that had kept him here so long.

Valerian took a deep breath and let it out in an aggrieved sigh.

No matter what the reason, no matter which excuse he chose to employ, here in the hallway he would remain, like some caged, pacing tiger, his mind a muddled mess, waiting for the performance to begin in the center ring of the circus—or Allegra's newly designated bedchamber, which, to Valerian's mind, was much the same thing.

The door behind him opened, putting an end to his agitated travels up and down the hall carpet.

"She's calling for you, Valerian," Agnes Kittredge said, her tone grudging as she exited the bedchamber to stand in front of him in the hallway. Her displeasure at having to deliver such a message was clearly evident on her thin, pinched face.

"I somehow sensed that she would," Valerian returned, sighing.

"This Allegro person," Agnes persisted, "does she speak any English at all? How can she claim to be English and not know her mother tongue? Foreigners are such a contrary lot, refusing to learn our language. Mary has a lot to answer for, bless her departed soul, if this person truly is who you claim her to be."

Valerian, who felt he had already borne more than he should, and knew he was most probably going to have to bear a great deal more when he presently confronted Allegra, looked down at Agnes with minutely narrowed eyes.

"Are you suggesting I have foisted an impostor on

your brother? I hesitate to point this out, but if you were a man, madam, I should be obliged to meet you on a field of honor for such an insult.''

Agnes was quick to deny what she had so clearly implied, adding, ''All the girl spouts is popish gibberish, save for your name, and might I say that I consider it very strange indeed that you have gifted her with the casual use of your Christian title. And, oh yes—did you know the chit wears no stays? To my way of thinking, that's just another indication of her sadly uncivilized nature.''

Valerian passed over this outburst, not feeling quite up to a discussion of women's undergarments at the moment, and inclined his head toward the door. ''I believe you said Signorina Crispino was asking for me? I presume there is a maidservant inside, to act as chaperon?''

Agnes rolled her watery eyes, giving up the fight, if only for the moment. ''Betty is with her, yes. I will await you downstairs in the drawing room. Please tell me if the girl wishes us to send for a doctor.'' She brightened momentarily. ''Perhaps she needs to be bled. She does have a very high color, doesn't she?''

His hand already raised to knock on the door, Valerian shot Agnes an amused look that implied that he, a functioning member of the male species, found Allegra's ''high color'' to be more in the way of an attraction than a telltale sign of ill health. ''I'll be sure to ask your niece if she wishes her dearest aunt to call for the leeches, madam. Now,'' he added as the maid opened the door, ''if you'll excuse me, I believe I have kept the signorina waiting long enough.''

Entering the bedchamber, Valerian motioned for the maid to return to her seat in the far corner of the darkened room and approached the side of the high tester bed. "You rang, signorina? I am entirely at your command, not that you would have it any other way. Perhaps you would like me to plump your pillows? Or maybe I might toddle down to the kitchens and get you a bite to eat, for you must be famished after your performance."

Allegra peered across the room to see Betty's head already nodding as if the maid was almost asleep; then she smiled brightly up at Fitzhugh. "I *was* wonderful, wasn't I, Valerian? I have always been very good at stage-acting, although I much prefer to be singing. My goodness—are they always like that? My new family, you understand. They buzz so angrily, like bees all after the same flower."

"So the 'flower' in question decided a timely 'wilt' was in order, is that it? I'll say one thing for you, Allegra. You do know how to break up a conversation."

Allegra dismissed his words with a small wave of her hand. "Someone had to do something before they all came to blows—and it certainly didn't appear as if *you* were going to take control any time soon. Did you hear my *nonno,* Valerian? He still intends to make me his heir, even though he has not yet died as promised. Tell me, is a hundred thousand pounds a great deal of money? It is not so much in lire, although it is very generous, but my cousin Gideon seemed quite impressed with the figure."

"Let me put it this way, my dear. For a hundred

thousand pounds *I* might even be induced to offer for your hand—if I didn't already know you better, that is,'' Valerian told her, pulling up a chair so that he could rest his weary body. ''But that's enough idle chatter. I would like an explanation of your almost totally unaccented speech, young lady. Your English seems to have improved a hundredfold since our journey began in Naples.''

Allegra pushed herself up against the backboard of the bed, her smile wide and unaffected. ''Then you have noticed! How wonderful, for I have been working ever so hard to rid myself of any lingering accent. *Madre* had taught me very well, and it is only since her death that my English became lazy.''

That said, she changed the subject. ''Did you know, Valerian, that dearest Signorina Shackleford was returning home to London after fifteen years as governess to the children of one of Napoleon's many cousins? No, of course you didn't. Men never ask important questions like that, do they? All they want in a chaperon is a respectable-looking female who eats little and keeps her mouth shut.''

''I would dearly love to learn just where and how you formed that opinion, Allegra,'' Valerian remarked, ''but I will forgo the urge for the moment in order to learn more of your arrangement with Miss Shackleford. Max found her for us, as I recall, the same day he procured your passport. I should have known she wasn't just someone he chanced upon in the street. Please, go on.''

Allegra pulled a face at him, but answered anyway. ''Signorina Shackleford is a particular friend of *Un-*

cail Max's. She had been trapped in Napoli thanks to the war, you understand, and then could not bring herself to leave until the last little Bonaparte was raised. She is a very strict taskmaster, Signorina Shackleford is, but as I was very determined, and *Madre*'s lessons came back to me once I applied my mind to the exercise, she was kind enough in the end to kiss me good-bye and tell me I had developed into one of her most apt pupils. Isn't that nice? Valerian— do you think you could send down to the kitchens for some food? Fainting seems to make me extremely hungry.''

"*Breathing* seems to make you extremely hungry,'' Valerian complained absently, his mind still struggling with the information Allegra had already supplied. "Tell me, how did you apply yourself so assiduously to your studies while suffering from such extreme seasickness? Miss Shackleford told me you could barely lift your head from your pillow and were not up to entertaining visitors in your stateroom.''

Allegra's expressive hands came into play once more as she pushed his words aside. "Oh, that. It was only a tiny fib, actually, for I really do not much like to sail, but I could think of no reason to stay out of your way for the length of the trip. You sometimes get a very strange look in your eyes, Valerian, as if you would find the world a much more pleasant place without me. I decided I would not much care for being tossed overboard if I inadvertently did something to upset you.

"But in the evenings, after the sun was well down, Signorina Shackleford and I took the air outside our cabin, for I should never have been able to spend the entire trip locked within four walls, even if the food was plentiful, though not especially tasty. Besides, I wished to surprise you with my progress, as a gift for being so nice as to rescue me from those terrible Timoteos, and for introducing me to dearest Tony and Candie and Murphy and *Uncail* Max—and most especially for holding me so close while I bad my dearest Italy good-bye.

"Oh, dear. You've got that strange look in your eyes again, Valerian. Are you angry with me yet again? I should think you'd be pleased. I've improved my English, I've become a much better sailor, and I did not pester you with my presence aboard ship. Honestly, I begin to believe I shall never understand you. But that is of no matter now. Tell me—what do you think of my *madre*'s relatives. I really do value your opinion—above everything!"

"Oh, you do, do you? I see Miss Shackleford has also taught you it is always good to flatter a man if you wish him to be cooperative." Valerian leaned back in the chair, crossing one long leg over the other before giving her his answer. "Very well, I shall tell you what I think of the inhabitants of this little nest of toothless vipers."

He took a deep breath and began. "Gideon is a dedicated but woefully inept gamester who alternately loathes his mother and sponges from her. He would also sell her to any passing tinker if he could get a good price. To put it bluntly—if I were ever to be involved in a fight, I should not long for Gideon Kittredge to guard my back.

"Your aunt Agnes is an overweening, meddlesome blockhead who will fawn over you if necessary to keep her position in this household, but who privately curses your mother for not strangling you at birth. She is totally obsessed with her son, so that I should expect she'll be throwing him at your head before the day is out in order to gain back her longed-for inheritance through your marriage.

"Isobel is a painfully plain, spiteful child—not entirely without cause—who believes herself a great beauty. Whatever you do, Allegra, don't let her have the dressing of you.

"Lastly," he said, marveling at the way Allegra's eyes seemed to grow wider with his every word, "we come to your grandfather. Now here is an old man trying to use his granddaughter—please don't think he loves you, pet, for he loves only his cherry ripe, and perhaps the Prince Regent—to buy his way into Heaven. Of the lot of them, I think I like Duggy the least, for the rest of them are fairly up front with their vices. Now, tell me your impressions."

Allegra's lower lip jutted out as she prepared her answer. "I think," she said at last, sighing, "that *Cugino* Gideon is a very pretty boy, much like Bernardo, but with all the vices the silly shoemaker lacks. *Zia* Agnes I do not like at all, and not just because she calls me Allegro, as if I were a musical direction and not a person. *Cugina* Isobel is a sad little underfed creature, looking much like a bad morning while her brother resembles a good night. Did you take notice, Valerian—*Cugina* Isobel's teeth are so jumbled that it makes me think she did not grow them, but must have stood across the room and had someone toss them at her, so that she had to quickly catch them with her mouth as best she could.''

Valerian suppressed a chuckle as Allegra opened her mouth and moved her head from side to side, as imitating Isobel's teeth-catching technique. ''And your grandfather?''

Allegra's antics came to an abrupt stop. ''He is my *madre*'s father, and he broke her heart. He did not even have the courtesy to write back to my *papà* when he sent him word that she had died. I should hate him—I always *have* hated him.'' She gave a wholly Italian shrug, shaking her head. ''But now—''

''But now?''

''I think he is sincere in wishing to make amends for his shabby treatment of my *madre*. He plans to use me to make his sister and her children uncomfortable, I am not so silly as to not understand that, but I saw something else in his eyes—just for a moment, you understand—when I performed my little faint. He was very worried. Yes, even if you cannot like him, Valerian, I think I should like to watch my *nonno* for a while longer before I pass the judgment.''

Valerian stared at her for a long moment, his estimation of her intelligence rising another notch. ''And is that why you played the uncomprehending ignoramus downstairs earlier? So that you could learn your relatives' true opinions and motives?''

''*Chi non fa, non falla,* Valerian,'' she answered, smiling. ''He who does nothing makes no mistakes. *Uncail* Max told me to first see what he called the lay of the land before I showed myself to them.''

"*Uncail* Max?" Valerian remarked, realizing that he was feeling slightly abused by the thought that Allegra, whom he, at least intellectually, wished to move out of his life, had sought advice from someone other than himself. "My, that little Irishman does get around, doesn't he? What else did he tell you?"

"He also reminded me of another Italian warning. *Non Cercate i peli nell'uovo.* I should not go looking for hairs inside an egg. In other words—"

"In other words," Valerian interrupted, rising, "you should not go looking for trouble. Hence the propitious swoon. All right, Allegra, I believe I understand everything now, an admittance that frightens me more than you know. I think enough time has passed for you to have recovered your senses. Would you like to rejoin the family? It is, after all, nearing the dinner hour."

At his last words Allegra sat forward quickly and swung her feet over the side of the bed, holding out a hand so that Valerian could help her descend from the high mattress to the floor. "I can only hope we will be having some of this famous roast beef Signorina Shackleford has told me about. It sounds delicious, although she says garlic is not a part of the dish. I can't imagine such uninspired cooking, but Signorina Shackleford says your English puddings are very nice. My *madre* never learned how to cook as a girl, so I have never eaten this bland-English before. You will stay to dinner, won't you, Valerian? I am ashamed to admit it, but my relatives frighten me, and I should be glad of your company for a while longer."

At the touch of her small hand, Valerian's best intentions took to their heels yet again and he found himself agreeing to her proposal. "But do not expect me to become your permanent champion, Allegra," he warned in self-defense. "I have been away from my estate for over two years, and must get on about my business as soon as possible."

Allegra gave a dismissive toss of her head. "If you have left it this long, Valerian, I should think one of two things has happened. Either your estate has been raped by your manager and fallen into rack and ruin, or it has prospered in your absence, which would mean you are not needed there at all. No matter which it is, I don't see that one little dinner can make much difference."

Opening the door to the hallway, Valerian acknowledged her maddeningly logical comment with a slight nod of his head, adding, "Polite English-women—polite women everywhere—do not employ the use of the word 'rape.' Although I know what you meant, some words, Allegra, do suffer in translation. Kindly remember that in future, please."

"I will remember, Valerian," she said meekly, although her sapphire eyes twinkled.

He pulled her unresisting arm through his and they began the descent to the first floor of the town house. "Now quickly, Allegra, before we rejoin the family— to what great miracle do we credit our sudden discovery of your mastery of the English language?"

"AND SO, DEAREST *NONNO,* you see it was all very silly of me," Allegra said from her perch on the foot-stool at Baron Dugdale's feet, "but my extreme excitement at finally meeting my beloved mother's family caused all of my carefully learned English to totally desert me. *Pouf!* Why, if I hadn't fainted, I don't know what would have happened.''

''I can only suppose, cousin, that you would have heard my dear, distraught mother call you vile names a dozen times rather than the mere half dozen you did hear,'' Gideon put in smoothly from his position across the room, leaning negligently against the marble mantelpiece.

''Gideon, you're such a cold, heartless wretch,'' Isobel inserted from her seat on the settee. ''Really, Mama, I don't know why you can't see straight through him.''

''All I see,'' Agnes returned forcefully, staring directly at the back of Allegra's head, ''is that this young woman, this Allegro, has descended on our peaceful home, and within the space of a single afternoon all the rest of its inhabitants are at each other's throats, saying vile, hurtful things to each other, even threatening each other with the loss of all the things in life that mean the most to them.''

''Allegra—with an A at each end,'' Allegra correctly sweetly, turning to face her aunt. ''Forgive me for bringing it to your attention, *Zia* Agnes, but I know you shouldn't like to address me incorrectly.''

''*'Zia* Agnes' don't want to address you at all,'' Gideon put in from his new position behind the settee. He had the most unnerving habit of moving about without making a sound, almost, Allegra thought, like a snake sliding through deep grass. ''You've given her—indeed, all of us—quite a turn, you know. We always thought we was Uncle's heirs.''

"There must be half a score of sharpers holding your vowels that will be likewise displeased to hear of Allegra's existence, once the word gets out,'' Lord Dugdale put in, chuckling into his cravat. "For your sake, nevvie, and the sake of your still intact knees, I hope you haven't been playing too deep on your expectations.''

"Denny, please!'' Agnes pleaded, her hands flying to her scrawny breast.

Lord Dugdale leaned down to address his granddaughter. "The boy was counting heavily on me sticking my spoon in the wall, you know, and then gleefully gambling away my life's savings within a fortnight. Queered him good, I did, by living, and I shouldn't be surprised to wake up dead one morning just so's he can make good on his markers.''

He looked up at Valerian. "You'll be my witness, boy. If I come to an untimely end before I can have my will changed over to benefit this sweet girl here, can I count on you to take Gideon's name to the nearest magistrate?''

Agnes gasped and quickly began fanning herself with a small lace handkerchief. "I don't think I can bear much more of this. Truly I don't.''

Allegra reached out to place a hand on the Baron's knee. "There is no need to trouble Valerian, *Nonno,*'' she said, her voice deceptively gentle. "If you should die before your time, I would make the *vendetta* and go directly to *Cugino* Gideon myself and slice out his ungrateful heart with a kitchen knife. We Italians are a bloodthirsty lot when it comes to family, you know.''

Agnes gave a single, ladylike shriek. ''Did you hear that! We shan't any of us be safe in our beds! Denny, you must do something at once—or else I shall be forced to quit this roof before nightfall.''

The Baron looked askance at his sister, who was clinging to her rigidly resisting daughter as if to protect her from the heathen in the midst. ''If only I could believe that, Agnes, I should rise from this chair this very moment and do a lively jig. But you are as firmly entrenched here as this damnable gout is in my big toe. Now if the lot of you would please be quiet, I wish to speak further with my granddaughter.''

''Speak with your granddaughter, then, you heartless creature,'' Agnes retorted, struggling to rise, ''but don't expect me to sit here and listen!''

''Mama, reconsider, please,'' Isobel begged, tugging at her mother's shawl as the older woman made to rise. ''You cannot be so rude to our new-found cousin''—she looked up at Valerian, her heart in her eyes—''or to our guest.''

''Oh, Mama, do sit down,'' Gideon ordered in disgusted tones. ''You know you wouldn't miss a word of what Uncle Denny has to say—no matter how much he insults you.''

''*Basta!*'' Allegra interrupted just as Valerian was beginning to feel that Waterloo, when compared with the scene in the Dugdale drawing room, could only be described as a slight skirmish. ''Enough! I wish for *everyone* to sit down—now—for *I* have something to say!''

Valerian's lips twitched appreciatively as all three Kittredges subsided into chairs, their attention directed to Allegra as she fussed momentarily with her skirts, prolonging the newly fallen silence until she felt her audience was ready to hear her speak. She was a minx all right, he knew, but he couldn't help but feel proud of her at this moment.

"Now, *Nonno, Zia* Agnes, Isobel—and you too, Gideon," she began at last, looking piercingly from one to the other as she spoke, "I would have to be blind and deaf not to feel the strain my appearance has caused to come to this family, and I have decided it is time we cleaned the air."

"Cleared the air, imp," Valerian corrected, his eyes flashing her a warning as he deliberately tried to keep her from saying anything in haste that she might repent later.

"Cleared the air, yes. Thank you, Valerian," she said tightly before turning back to her relatives. "Now, where was I? First of all, I think you should know more about me, as I am a stranger to you. For one, my disposition is not always so calm—"

"I can vouch for that," Valerian slid in neatly, propping himself against the side of Lord Dugdale's high wing chair, his arms crossed against his chest.

Allegra shot him a look guaranteed to freeze lava if it should ever again dare to descend from Vesuvius. "I am also, when sufficiently pushed, malicious enough to strike back twofold for any injury I sustain."

"I can vouch for that as well," Valerian agreed happily as Allegra continued to glare at him. "But if it's any consolation to you, Agnes, she doesn't spit anymore.''

"Don't pay him any attention, *Nonno*,'' Allegra cautioned her grandfather. And then she smiled as inspiration struck. "You see, Valerian is just angry because I refuse to love him.''

"I'm what?'' Valerian, who had thought he was at last prepared for anything Allegra might say or do—and who had actually believed himself to be in charity with her only a second earlier—belatedly closed his mouth and fought the urge to strangle the little vixen on the spot.

"Don't bother to deny it, Valerian." Allegra's lips twitched at his outburst and she lowered her gaze—not seeing the strange, cold look that had crept into Isobel's watery hazel eyes.

Gideon, however, noticed his sister's involuntary flinch, and he did not bother to hide his glee. "How titillating, dear Cousin Allegra," he crooned, his mouth just beside Isobel's ear as he leaned over the settee. "Do go on."

Allegra shot Gideon a withering look, then turned back to her grandfather. "It is true. Valerian is deeply in love with me—as are so many men; a circumstance I find very troubling to my tender heart. But, alas, I cannot love Valerian, or any man. I am, you see, completely dedicated to my art.''

"You draw pictures?" Lord Dugdale questioned blankly as Isobel—unnoticed again by any save her brother, who made a habit of storing up miscellaneous information he could possibly put to some malicious use at a later date—raised a hand to her mouth and bit down hard on her knuckle. "What do you draw, child? Pictures of castles and the like? I guess that's all right. Prinny favors faces, though, and horses. Can you draw horses?"

"I do not draw, *Nonno*," Allegra answered patiently, still purposely avoiding Valerian's sure-to-be-condemning eyes. He might have warned her against it, but she had to tell the truth. "I sing. Like my *papà* before me, I am a great singer. People pay money to hear me sing. I tell you this, not because I am proud, but because I wish you to know that I do not need your conscience money. If you were to disown me today as you disowned my *madre* twenty years ago, I should not starve. Orphan that I am, I can make my own way."

Gideon came around the settee to sit down beside his mother. "Well, good. She's a resourceful puss, unlike my dear sister, who can only embroider slippers—and only ones with the same name on them at that. It's settled, then. Cousin Allegra is to set herself up as the town warbler. But don't think we're completely without compassion, dearest cousin. You may still stay for dinner."

"Gideon," Isobel said quietly.

"Yes, sister mine? Is there something you require?" the young man responded, grinning widely in appreciation of his own humor.

"Yes, there is. I'd like your silence, Gideon," Isobel suggested succinctly, her thin, sallow face so pinched it reminded Allegra mightily of a Tuscany olive left too long in the sun.

At this point, and high time it was for the man to

make a move, Baron Dugdale took the conversational bit firmly beneath his teeth. "Odds fish, but she's got all her mother's fire! Mary was my daughter to the bone—and a rare handful, which should have told me that once she'd made up her mind to marry that *I*-talian bloke, I shouldn't have tried to stop her. Well, the apples don't fall that far from the tree, like they say, and what you get with the mother you're just as likely to see in the daughter. I'm going to enjoy you, Allegra, even though we probably will fight like cats in a sack most of the time."

"Thank you, *Nonno*," Allegra said, feeling the threat of tears behind her eyes for the first time since she had left Naples. "But please don't think I wish more than a roof over my head. I can make my own way without having you push *Zia* Agnes and her children out into the gutter."

"If that's where they belong, then that's where they'll land," the Baron answered shortly, glaring at his sister. "But if they behave themselves—" He allowed this last sentence to dangle, waiting for Agnes to pick up his hint.

He didn't have long to wait. "I have never been known to be less than civil, Denny," she said, lifting her pointy chin. "If you wish me to take Mary's child under my wing, I shall be happy to do so. What is it you want me to do? Educate her in the ways of polite society? Teach her the intricacies of acceptable behaviour and prudent speech? Introduce her to the finer points of modest dress—to *stays?*"

"Stays?" Lord Dugdale ejaculated, his gaze resting on Allegra's remarkably fine figure. "What would she be wanting to truss herself up like a Christmas goose for, I ask you? If it's her chest that's bothering you, Aggie, I think you're fair and far out there. She has a lovely chest—probably comes from all those deep breaths singers take, don't you think, Valerian? Valerian? Now where the devil did the fellow go?''

They all looked to where Valerian had been standing just a few moments earlier, but he wasn't there. Without his dinner, without bidding any of them farewell, he had gone.

"How rude!" Agnes exclaimed, aghast.

"Oh, dear. Do you think Cousin Allegra's silly remarks upset him?" Isobel questioned, her voice hopeful.

"He was aboard ship a long time. Probably decided he needs a woman," Gideon offered helpfully, if only to watch his sister's thin cheeks go pale.

"A woman, is it, nevvie?" the Baron snorted. "And what would you be knowing of women—you who never got close to any save the Queen of Hearts?"

As the Kittredges and her grandfather launched themselves into yet another argument, Allegra sat on the footstool, staring into the middle distance, a decidedly pleased smile on her face.

For Allegra knew where Valerian had gone. He had gone to ground, in order to get away from her. But he would be back. Oh, yes. One way or the other, he would be back.

CHAPTER FIVE

IT TOOK slightly less than three days for Allegra, always a highly emotional girl, to fall totally in love with Brighton. The bracing sea air that made her feel so alive, the crash of the surf, the winding streets and lovely narrow houses—all this and more Allegra enjoyed during her lengthy daily walks along the Steine with a grumbling Betty in tow, complaining that she would doubtless have to spend the remainder of her wretched life brushing crusted sea salt out of her new mistress's hair.

But more than anything else, Allegra had fallen under the enchantment of the Prince Regent's Marine Pavilion. It reminded her of a snow-white castle out of some marvelous fairy tale, a glorious confection of swirling onion-shaped domes, pinnacles, minarets, and intricate lacelike embattlements that seemed too delicate, too ethereally beautiful to be real.

But even more than the sea air or the neat houses or even the fantasylike Pavilion, Allegra fell in love with the Prince Regent. She had not seen him, of course, for he was in seclusion, only a few months having passed since the tragic childbed deaths of his daughter, the Princess Charlotte of Wales, and his grandson, and no one really saw him.

Allegra loved him because he was suffering, and her emotional Italian heart felt a high degree of *simpatia* for a man in mourning. But she felt even more in charity with him because Prinny, no matter what his faults, loved music. He loved music so much that, even in his grief, he allowed his most excellent German musicians to play outside on the Pavilion grounds in order to entertain the citizens. Allegra had been immediately enthralled to hear the great works of composers such as Bach, Haydn, and Beethoven wafting through the windblown trees, and when the band broke into a familiar Italian *sinfonia,* she ached with the desire to hum along.

But if she had learned nothing else in her first days in Brighton, Allegra had learned it was not wise to call too much attention to herself. Brighton might be lovely, but the people she met along the Steine were very strange indeed. They were displaced Londoners all, Betty had told her, hangers-on of the Prince Regent who would follow the great man to the ends of the earth, simply for an invitation to the Pavilion.

Mostly older, the women were a sad, over-stuffed collection of molting peahens, while the gentlemen seemed to vary in age but no inclination, eyeing Allegra as a hungry wolf would eye a spring lamb. The younger women who passed by, some of them with faces painted as if for the stage, were, according to Betty, "milliners." Allegra, although not familiar with English customs, had no difficulty in understanding that these ladies' closest proximity to bonnets came about only when they were wearing them.

Betty, who had lived in Brighton all her life, became a veritable fountain of information for Allegra, who could not seem to locate the bottom of her deep barrel of questions about the town in which her mother had grown up.

"She must have loved my *papà* very much, to leave such a wonderful place," Allegra said to Betty as they stood outside the Pavilion, watching as a weak sun glinted off the main onion dome and danced against the stained-glass windows.

Betty was quick to correct her. In 1796, the year Mary Catherine Dugdale had slipped down a rope made of knotted bed sheets and into the arms of her Italian lover, the Marine Pavilion had been little more than a discreetly amended farmhouse, a modest residence the Prince shared with Mrs. Maria Fitzherbert, "the lady he should have stuck with, rather than that terrible Lady Jersey or the naughty Princess Caroline, and most especially not any of those fat old hens that roost with him now."

Yes, according to Betty things were a lot different in 1796, even if the Prince's rowdy bachelor friends sometimes pulled silly pranks on the townspeople and kept everyone up half the night with their drinking and rowdy ways.

"It was that bad when that Lady Jersey got her hooks into him, missy," Betty told Allegra as they sat together in the latter's bedchamber near midnight of her fourth evening in England, the two of them rapidly having gone past the usual mistress-maid association. "It was Lady Jersey what stole the Prince from Mrs. Fitzherbert and then talked him into marrying that German person, who was mother to Princess Charlotte, Lord rest her dear soul. And where was her mother when poor Princess Charlotte breathed her last? Nowhere to be found, that's where!''

"Yes, Betty," Allegra responded, handing the maid a sugarplum. "I have already heard your opinion of Princess Caroline and her travels with her Italian Chamberlain. What I want to hear about is Brighton itself.''

"We had some hard times after your mother left. I blame it all on that terrible Lady Jersey, who started the fuss in the first place. You know, the people of Brighton so loved Mrs. Fitzherbert, and so disliked Lady Jersey, that when Lady Jersey's coach passed through the streets the citizens hissed at her and called her names. The Prince didn't much care for that, and the year your mother left he didn't even come to Brighton, but went to Bognor with his terrible lady. It was as if the whole world had forgotten us. Shops closed. People moved away. Your grandfather, the Baron, was so beside himself he nearly sold this house and moved to London. We all suffered mightily in the next four years, until he made it up with Mrs. Fitzherbert and came back to Brighton.''

"And is Signora Fitzherbert still here with the Prince?" Allegra asked, her mouth full of sugarplums as she sat cross-legged on the bed. "And if she is, who are all the fat ladies you mentioned?''

Betty screwed up her plain-as-pudding face. "Mrs. Fitzherbert is still here, but she finally had enough of the Prince's goings-on and refuses to see him.'' Betty leaned forward in her chair to impart quietly, "I hear he still wears a likeness of her in a locket around his neck, the silly old fool." She sat back once more, folding her arms. "But no, the Prince spends his time now with fat old women like that Lady Hertford and that other one before her, Lady Conyngham. He does not want a wife now, missy; he longs for a mother who will tell him that he is a good boy."

Allegra sniffed a time or two and wiped at a tear with the back of one hand. "He sounds so sad, Betty, and so alone. It must be terrible to be a prince forever when you long to be King. Oh, I know he must be a terrible man, but he loves beauty so much, in both form and music, that I cannot believe you English understand him. In Italy we have many great men— lovers of art and music and literature—who are not always very nice people. Why, just think of the Medici! That may be the price of genius, don't you think?"

Betty sniffed as well, but not to stifle the threat of tears. "My sister Clara once worked as housemaid at the Pavilion, missy. Clara told me she spent the whole of the time with her back to the wall so as not to be pinched by this genius of yours. No, missy," she ended firmly, "he should have stayed with Mrs. Fitz- herbert. She knew how to keep him in line. But you'll see it all for yourself soon enough, I wager. The Baron is one of the Prince's closest chums here in Brighton, and the whole lot of you will probably be going over there for dinner any time now."

This brought Allegra's attention away from the Prince and onto one of her favorite subjects: food. Valerian had already told her a little about the enormous feasts that lasted for hour upon hour, and she looked forward to an evening in the great Pavilion's Banqueting Room.

"One hundred and sixteen separate dishes for a single banquet, Betty!" she exclaimed, rubbing her flat belly. "All eaten beneath a huge chandelier suspended from the claws of a ferocious dragon clinging to a plantain tree on the ceiling! Oh, yes, *Nonno* has already told me a great deal about this magnificent Banqueting Room. It all sounds so grand that I cannot believe the Prince Regent is English. There must be a secret Florentine lurking about somewhere in his family tree, to have him love beauty and food so much."

"If there is, I wouldn't mention it to your grandfather," the maid advised, reaching for one last sugarplum. "From what I've heard below-stairs, even though he's that tickled to have you here with him, he still isn't so happy with anything *I*-talian."

Allegra popped the last sugarplum into her mouth, then leaned forward, squinting at the maid. "What have you heard, Betty? The terrible Kittredges don't worry me, but I should not like to think my *nonno* is still harboring a grudge against my poor *papà*."

Betty's dark eyes slid away from Allegra's searching gaze. "Nothing, missy, I heard nothing. At least nothing important. Just something about how he missed you and your mother all those years you were traipsing all over that heathen country like a band of gypsies, following your da from one place to next just so's he could sing. That's all. Yes, I'm sure now that was the whole of it. My, it's late, missy. Would you like for me to turn down your bed?''

''Betty?'' Allegra felt ill suddenly, which might have been due to the niggling feeling that something she wasn't going to like was about to happen. It also could have been due to the fact that, between them, they had succeeded in eating an entire candy dish full of sugarplums, but Allegra didn't think so.

''Yes, missy?'' Betty was looking decidedly pale as she fidgeted in her chair.

''My *nonno* sent a note to me this evening, saying he wishes for me to meet with him in his study after luncheon tomorrow. I thought we were going to talk about *Madre* again, as we have done every day since I arrived. We aren't going to be talking about her tomorrow, are we?''

Betty rose and made a great business out of whisking bits of sugar from the satin bedspread. ''Please, missy, don't ask me to say more, because I really don't know. The Baron had his solicitor here this afternoon and Bates, one of the footmen, heard the master cursing and yelling about *I*-talians. So I don't really know why he wants to see you or what the two of you will be talking about.'' She straightened up and looked her new mistress, her new friend, straight in the eye. ''I only feel sure you probably aren't going to like it. I'm that sorry, missy. Truly I am.''

THE NEXT MORNING dawned gray and misty, with a fog rolling in from the ocean. The weather matched Allegra's mood, for she had spent a restless night wondering about her grandfather's summons, only to fall into a fitful sleep near dawn that included a strange dream in which Valerian Fitzhugh figured prominently.

They had been running through the streets of Brighton, she and Valerian, with some unknown assailant hard on their heels. It was very dark, so that no matter how often Allegra looked behind her, it was impossible to learn the identity of their pursuer. Her hand clasped tightly in Valerian's, all she could do was run, and keep on running, even though she was singing an aria at the top of her lungs at the same time.

Then the scene had changed, and Allegra had seen herself standing at the end of a long aisle, her arm through that of her smiling grandfather as he led her toward a candlelit altar. How lovely! She was to be a bride! As she walked along she strained to make out the identity of her groom, but just as she thought she was close enough to discern his features, a great wind roared through the church, blowing out all the candles and plunging the interior into complete darkness.

"Sing, Allegra!" a voice cried to her from the altar. "Sing, and I shall find you."

Allegra, her grandfather mysteriously gone from her side, opened her mouth to sing, but nothing happened. She had no voice, no way to signal to her groom.

"Throw coins, Allegra!" a second voice commanded from the altar. "Throw coins, and by their lovely jingle I shall find you."

Allegra reached into her pockets to find some

coins, but all she found there were sugarplums. Dozens and dozens of sugarplums. Desperate, she flung them in the general direction of the altar.

"I'll tap, Allegra!" called a third voice, this time in Italian. "I'll tap my little hammer so that you can find me. First I'll tap on the head of your *maestro*, and then I shall tap on the head of this silly gamester. Tap, tap, tap, until I find you, *mi amore*."

"*Bernardo!*" Allegra had awakened then, drenched in perspiration, the shoemaker's name bursting from her lips before she could clap a hand over her mouth. She rested her throbbing head in her hands. "What a terrible nightmare," she said, moaning as she slid from the bed to get a drink of water from the pitcher that stood on a table at the far side of the bedchamber.

After a leisurely breakfast in bed, as Betty helped her to bathe and dress, Allegra was still troubled by the dream. The first part of it was easily explained, probably nothing more than a delayed reaction to her months of flight round Italy to avoid Bernardo and her rescue by Valerian.

Also easily explained was the groom who wished her to throw money. He could be none other than Gideon. As she had already recognized Bernardo by both his voice and the words "little hammer," she was puzzled only about the identity of the groom who commanded her to sing.

She would have very much liked to believe that it had been Valerian, but he had time and again warned her against singing—he, who had never so much as heard her hum. "Which probably explains why I couldn't sing for him—if it was him,'' she said aloud as Betty stood behind her, buttoning the last of the buttons on the buttercup-yellow muslin morning gown.

''Pardon, missy?'' Betty asked, turning Allegra about to inspect the evenness of the hem. ''Who would you be singing to at this hour of the morning?''

''Who indeed?'' Allegra answered without answering, moving past Betty to check her appearance in the mirror above the japanned dresser. The reflection that met her eyes pleased her. Betty, bless her, had a wonderful way with long hair, so that Allegra's ebony tresses had been tamed without losing their vibrant life. The yellow muslin was demurely cut, with two-inch-wide white lace ruching about the neckline that set off her pale skin to advantage.

She looked, even to her own eyes, extremely English—except perhaps for the dancing life in her lively sapphire eyes.

''Do I look presentable, Betty? Do I look like the good granddaughter?'' she asked, twirling about, holding her skirt away from her ankles.

''You look beautiful, missy,'' Betty replied, although she bit at her lower lip as if there was something about Allegra's appearance that bothered her. ''You forgot all about what I told you last night, didn't you, missy?''

Allegra blinked three times, then smiled. ''Forgot about what, Betty? Did you tell me something upsetting last night?''

Betty exhaled on a deep sigh. ''Thank you, missy. For a minute there you had a look in your eyes that—

well, never mind me. I'm just getting old, I suppose. I like my place in this household, even if Mrs. Kittredge can be as cheap as meat on a chicken neck. That is—I mean, I wouldn't want to leave you, missy. Not for worlds.''

''It's all right, Betty. There is nothing my *nonno* can do to upset me. I was alone and lost in Italy until he sent for me, and I am not so stupid as to refuse to be grateful. Besides, I am too happy in this beautiful place not to be in charity with the world. I promise I shall be on my very best behavior.''

Allegra skipped across the room to pat the maid's round cheek, then dashed out the door, eager for luncheon to be over and her meeting with the Baron to begin. She deliberately pushed any lingering thoughts of the past night's strange dream from her mind.

For three days her grandfather had pretty much left her to her own devices. For three days the Kittredges had been icily polite to her. But it would appear her lovely, carefree time of adjustment was about to come to an end.

Allegra passed another mirror in the upstairs hallway and glanced into it, wondering if Valerian Fitzhugh would approve of her ''English'' appearance. Then she shook her head back and squared her shoulders, deliberately pushing thoughts of Valerian—who still insisted upon hiding himself on his estate somewhere just outside a village called Pyecombe—to the back of her mind.

She had made a promise to Betty, a solemn promise between friends she sincerely believed she could keep, but she could not entirely fight off the feeling that she was going to need all of her wits about her for the next few hours.

"YOU ARE IMPERTINENT!"

"No!" Allegra rounded on her grandfather—her black-as-night curls swinging about her shoulders, her eyes flashing blue fire, her cheeks flushed with fury— looking every inch the hot-blooded, emotional Italian. "You are wrong! *I* am Allegra Crispino. *You, Nonno,* are impertinent!" She then launched herself into a stream of Italian that, had he been able to understand it, would have had her grandfather's sparse halo of hair standing on end.

"Knock, knock. A thousand apologies for what I can only see as my untimely interruption. I have arrived at a bad time, haven't I? Haven't you fed her yet? She growls more on an empty stomach, you know. My goodness, but I think my ears are burning. Duggy—I'm surprised all the paint hasn't blistered right off these walls. What's going on in here that our little Italian fishwife has come to the conclusion that your parents neglected to exchange marriage vows?"

Allegra and the Baron turned as one to see Valerian Fitzhugh lounging against the doorjamb, one leg crossed over the other at the ankle.

"Valerian!" Allegra exclaimed, running to his side to drag him willy-nilly into the room. "It has been so long. I thought we might only see you every death of a pope."

"Fitzhugh, thank God!" Baron Dugdale bellowed from his seat, his bandaged foot propped on a footstool in front of him. "Odds fish, but I'm glad you're here. You speak her lingo. Maybe you can talk some sense into the gel.''

Valerian disengaged himself from Allegra's grasp, not without some difficulty, and sat himself down in the leather chair facing the Baron's. ''Do I have to, Duggy? I have been enjoying my homecoming, believing you and Allegra to be agreeably settled. It would pain me unbearably if you were to undeceive me now by telling me that something is amiss.''

Allegra dropped to her knees in front of him, her yellow muslin skirt billowing out to make her look as if she were sitting in a soft puddle of spring sunshine, and put her hands on his knees. ''Valerian, you are this moment to stop amusing yourself at my expense!'' she commanded tightly, her grammar slipping a notch in her agitation. ''This is a very serious thing we have to discuss.''

Valerian very deliberately wiped the smile from his face. ''Oh, we are to be serious, Allegra? What terrible thing has your grandfather done—cut back on your rations?''

''Food! Always it is food with you. Can't you think of anything else? And don't be stupid, Valerian. *Nonno* would never starve me. He would only *kill* me! He would only tear my heart into little pieces!'' She turned her head to shoot a quick, angry look at her grandfather, then continued. ''He has ordered me to call myself Crispin. Allegra *Crispin!* He wishes for me to forget I am Italian, to forget my *papà!*''

Valerian looked down at Allegra, saw the tears standing brightly in her deep blue, soul-wrenching eyes, and then raised his head to confront the Baron. "Is this true, Duggy?"

"Odds bobs, of course it's true!" the man exclaimed hotly. "Had my solicitor in here yesterday, you know, to change my will, but I couldn't do it. It stuck in my craw to put the name Crispino in it. What kind of a name is that—Crispino? Damned *I*-talian nonsense, throwing vowels around like pebbles in a brook. My granddaughter is English. Now, *Crispin*— that's a good English name. Nothing to be ashamed of in a Crispin, eh?"

Valerian felt the muscles in his shoulders tightening as he longed to jump up and push his fist squarely into Dennis Dugdale's ignorant face. Instead, he pinned a small smile on his features. "Being just a bit of a prig, aren't you, Duggy? I mean, it is only one letter."

"Only one letter? Only one letter! *Stupido!*" Allegra hopped to her feet, her bosom heaving in her agitation as she began to pace. "It is not only a letter! I am my *papà*'s daughter as well as my *madre*'s. He would ask me to give up my *papà*, Valerian, as if that sainted man never existed. No! I will not have it. *Viaggio come un baule.* I have traveled like a trunk, taken a trip from Italy to England, and gained nothing from the experience! I do not call having my heart stepped upon a gain. No! I have made up my mind, and you cannot change it. I am very sorry for it, for I have come to like this place, and I will miss Betty, to whom I have broken my solemn promise, but I must return to Italy."

"Tell her she can't do that, Valerian," the Baron

piped up, trying to move his unwieldly bulk about in the chair so that he could see Allegra, who had moved to the window. "Tell her she has to stay with me. A plum, Valerian—I'm giving her a plum. Doesn't the child understand that?"

"*Basta!*" Valerian watched as Allegra reversed her direction, to run back to her grandfather. Leaning down so that her hands rested on the armrests on either side of him, she spoke directly into his face. "A plum is money, *Nonno*. Only money. And you are giving it to me only in order to spite your sister and her children. I had thought it might be different— hoped it might be different—but it is not. You are a horrible, hateful old man, just like Valerian said, and I hope that when you do meet Saint Peter, he orders you thrown into the deepest, darkest pit in all of Hades."

The Baron cringed, as if trying to burrow into the back of the chair, and swallowed hard. "Now, Allegra," he began in a small voice, "you must remember. I am not a well man. I could die at any time. Did—did Fitzhugh really say that?"

"Never mind what he said!" Still hovering over him, her eyes shooting sparks of blue fire, she said, slowly and distinctly, "In Italy we have a saying. *Quando nascono sono tutti belli, quando si maritano, tutti buoni e quando muoiono, tutti santi.* What I have said, *Nonno*, is that people, when they are born, all are beautiful; when they marry, they are all good; and when they die, they are all saints."

"That—that's a very nice saying, Allegra," the Baron squeaked, still trying to burrow into the back of the chair. "Fitzhugh? You still there?" he called softly, as if for help.

"No, *Nonno,* it is not *nice.* Not all babies are beautiful, nor are all brides good. Most especially, death does not turn a sinner into a saint. We would all like to believe it to be so, but it is not true. You, *Nonno,* have made yourself a bid for sainthood, but you have failed. You are a terrible, nasty, self-serving old sinner. Dying won't change that, or make the world remember you differently.

"Now I know why my *madre* could leave this beautiful Brighton. And now I know why she sometimes cried at night. Not for you, *Nonno*—it could never have been for you. She cried for Brighton. For her beloved England. I have enough English blood in my veins to love this place myself. But you ask too much, *Nonno,* and you do not ask it for the right reasons. *Now* do you understand?"

Valerian, who had just moments earlier believed Allegra might completely lose control of her emotions and begin throwing things, settled back in his own chair and clapped his hands together softly. "I may live to be proud of you yet, imp," he said as Allegra whirled about to face him.

She was suddenly all smiles as she turned her head in Valerian's direction. "Then you agree with me, Valerian?"

He rose to stand looking down at her. "Do I agree that you should be allowed to return to Italy? No, I cannot agree with that, for it is a very long swim and I doubt you can afford to pay for your passage. Do I agree that you should be allowed to keep the surname given to you by your father? Yes, I most certainly do. Lastly, do I agree that your grandfather, your *nonno,* is a sure candidate for an eternity of hellfire and brimstone? Oh, yes, imp, I most assuredly do agree. I might even go so far as to say I endorse it."

"You too, Fitzhugh?" The Baron's bottom lip jutted out and he allowed his chin—both his chins—to fall onto his egg-stained cravat. "Odds fish, I never thought one little letter could cause such a fuss. I am a fool, Allegra. A stupid, stubborn old fool. Very well, then. You may keep your name—and my fortune. Only please, granddaughter—don't leave me. You're the only member of my Mary that I have left."

The old man's self-pitying tone was Allegra's undoing. Abandoning her threatening stance, she threw herself at the Baron's neck, giving him a resounding kiss on the cheek. "Ah, *Nonno,* I am such a terrible person myself. Truly, I did not mean it when I said you had the scruples of a hungry shark. Nor do I really wish for your big toe to blow up like a pig bladder and burst, or for a wart the size of a melon to grow on the very tip of your nose, or for—"

"I think the Baron accepts your apology, imp," Valerian interrupted. "You don't have to give him a recital of all the nastiness you were wishing on him when I arrived."

Allegra stepped back from the chair, smoothed her hair, and folded her hands together in front of her, somehow managing to look as innocent as a novitiate about to take the veil. "You're right, of course, Valerian, although I know my behavior was most shameful.'' She looked up, her sapphire eyes twinkling so that he could see a flash of her usual fire peeping out at him. ''But I was much provoked, wasn't I, Valerian?''

''Yes, imp. You were much provoked,'' Valerian agreed as Allegra once more took up what seemed to be her usual position, perched on the edge of the Baron's footstool. He looked piercingly at the older man. ''Now tell us, Duggy, do you have any more little surprises in store for your granddaughter, or can I leave now, secure in the knowledge that Allegra won't be wishing for a very large, very heavy brick house to fall on your head any time soon? Italian curses can be the very devil, you know.''

The Baron made a great business out of picking a stray piece of breakfast ham from the folds of his cravat. ''Well, boy, now that you mention it—there is one other thing. That's why I sent for you in the first place. You will help me, just to show that the gel here was wrong and you don't really think I'm a bad man?''

Allegra smiled in delight, for anything that would keep Valerian—who had championed her plea to retain her identity—nearby could not possibly serve to upset her.

The Baron coughed once, and continued. ''It's Aggie, Valerian. She's cutting up stiff about taking Allegra here to her dressmaker and all those other places women go to spend my money. Seems to think the girl's figure is an embarrassment, or some such drivel. Isobel offered to escort her cousin, but I'm not so daft as to let that one have the dressing of her.''

Valerian conjured up a mind picture of the underfed, overdressed Isobel of the crooked teeth. "Really," he said, desperately trying not to pay attention to the comical face Allegra was making at that moment.

"Think about it, Valerian. M'niece considers herself a beauty, you know, when even an old man like me can see she's as scrawny as a wind-burned dead tree, so it's sure as check she thinks Allegra here is some freak of nature. Why, I heard her just yesterday, telling Aggie that what this girl here needs is to have her hair all cut off and gowns that button to her chin."

Valerian looked down at Allegra, seeing the creamy expanse of skin that peeped out above the neckline of her gown and feeling a sharp shaft of envy at the familiarity with which her heavy black curls caressed her gently sloping shoulders. "Madness," he said softly.

"Madness, indeed! And I won't have it, you understand!" he ended, slapping his knee for emphasis, which set up a terrible throbbing in his badly swollen toe. "Damme, but that hurts like the very devil! Valerian—you have to do something. We're to go to the Pavilion Thursday night!"

Valerian reluctantly tore his attention away from Allegra's bodice, which rose and fell ever so slightly with her every breath. "I'm afraid I don't have a cure for gout stuffed in my pocket, Duggy. Sorry." Valerian refused to even seriously consider the Baron's outrageous request concerning Allegra. It was too dangerous, for both of them.

Allegra, for her part, had become awash with sev-

eral different emotions as her grandfather spoke. She
knew herself to be tinglingly aware of Valerian's
presence, standing as he was, so close behind her that
if she were only to lean back the slightest bit, her
spine would make contact with his knee.

She had been thrilled to think that a reason had
been found to keep Valerian by her side, then immediately confused to think that she wanted him by
her side for any other reason than to torment him for
bringing her to England and then abandoning her.

She had been hurt, but only mildly, as she listened
to her female relatives' opinions of her. She had been
also hurt, most severely, by Valerian's obtuse and
most obvious skirting of the Baron's request for assistance. And lastly, she had been struck by her
grandfather's obvious pain.

Putting all else aside, she asked, "Are you eating
the *ciliegie, Nonno*—that is, lots and lots of cherries?
Deep red cherries are the best kind. There was a music master we met once in Gargano who swore by
them to relieve the swelling of gout. *Zia* Agnes surely
has you eating cherries. And no pepper, *Nonno*. Pepper is very bad for your toe, I think."

Dugdale looked at his granddaughter, tears forming
in his eyes. "Did you hear that, Valerian? She's an
angel, an angel sent to me in my affliction. Cherries,
eh? I like cherries. Now why didn't Aggie know that?
Do you think we can get any cherries here in Brighton
this time of year?"

Allegra knew opportunity when it struck and, to her
mind, it was banging most mightily on the door at
precisely that moment. She sprang to her feet, grab-

bing onto Fitzhugh's forearm. "Valerian will know just where to go, won't you, Valerian? Why, we shall leave this very moment, just as soon as I fetch my wrap, and scour Brighton from one end to the other until we find cherries. And if we should find a dress shop or two along the way so that I might discover some gown suitable for wearing when dining beneath a chandelier held by a dragon, well, wouldn't that be above everything wonderful?"

Before Valerian knew what had hit him—actually, he knew what had hit him but found himself unable to resist either Allegra's enthusiasm or the chance to be with her for just a little while—the two of them were going out the door.

CHAPTER SIX

ALLEGRA CLUNG closely—dared he stay *too* closely?—to Valerian's arm as they walked along the
windblown Steine, the first part of their mission ac-
complished. It had taken inquiries at six different
shops, and her refusal of one basket of hothouse-
grown cherries as being entirely too hard for her liking, but at last Allegra had pronounced herself satisfied.

Valerian had paid for a clerk to deliver the fruit to
Number 23—and paid for the cherries as well, as
Dugdale did not keep an account at that particular
shop—and now they were merely walking and talking, enjoying the day.

If anyone had told Valerian that he could take pleasure in window shopping with a young miss not yet
out of her teens, listening to her chatter about ribbons
and flounces and the merits of silk linings, he would
most probably have laughed out loud. Yet he knew
himself to be happy in Allegra's company.

Now that he thought of it, he was almost always
happy in Allegra's company. Or angry. Or amused.
Or confused. Well, at least he was never bored. She
was an intelligent little minx, well traveled—if only
in Italy—and not in the least bit missish or shy. She

seemed to be endlessly delighted with everything and everybody, and Valerian found himself thinking how wonderful it would be to repeat his tour of Europe with her by his side.

"Cold, imp?" he asked as Allegra gave a delicate shiver. "Ladies usually shun walking for carriages in February, you know."

She looked up at him, the brim of her green velvet bonnet grazing his shoulder, and he could see that the wind had brought a flattering bloom to her cheeks. "Do they really, Valerian? I have always liked to ride on San Francesco's horse—which you know means to go on foot, as did the good Saint Francis. What a shame your English ladies do not like walking, when it is so very invigorating to face down the elements."

"Always looking for another challenge, aren't you, Allegra? I imagine you'll be trying the bathing machines one of these days."

"Oh, yes, indeed. Betty has told me all about them, and this woman, this very strong Martha Gunn, who dips ladies into the water. I love the seaside, don't you? But I think I most love to look out over the ocean and think of the places that lie beyond the water, the people who live there, the wonderful sights I could see. Valerian—have you ever traveled to America? We discovered it, you know. We Italians, that is. Our Christoforo Colombo, in 1492, I believe—although the silly Spanish like to take credit for it, of course. Isn't that always the way of it?"

Valerian's lips twitched in amusement. "The silly Spanish might have thought that, as they had put down the money for the project, they deserved some recognition. And no, I haven't yet traveled to what we still would like to call our colonies. Would you like to go to America, Allegra?''

"Oh, my, yes!" she exclaimed, skipping a bit as they passed over an uneven patch of flagway. ''I have wanted with all my heart to tour in America—singing, you know—and in Paris, and in Vienna, and in Moscow, and maybe even in faraway Japan, where women do not sing.'' Her face fell and she added, "But I never shall, I suppose, or at least not for many years to come. For now I must be a supporting prop to *Nonno,* and then later, well—how could I enjoy myself on my poor dead *nonno*'s money?''

"You couldn't, could you?'' Valerian directed their steps to a wooden bench along the side of the flagway. Once they were seated and he could see into her eyes, he asked, "What do you intend to do with your inheritance then, imp? Stuff it into boxes and bury it all in the back garden?''

She lifted her chin in what, to him, was now her easily recognizable expression of defiance. "And what good would that do? You are making sport of me, Valerian, and I don't think that is very nice. No, I have already decided what I shall do once dear *Nonno* is gone—which I can only hope will not be for a very, very long time. I shall take just enough money to keep myself until I can find employment as a singer, and give the rest to my *zia* Agnes.''

"You're going to do *what!*'' It was a good thing Valerian was sitting down, for he otherwise probably would have fallen, giving himself a nasty bump on his head while he was about it.

He longed to throttle her. How could he feel so in charity with this infuriating child one minute and long to strangle her the next? "Are you telling me that I gave up my trip and dragged you all the way to England just so you could turn up your nose at a fortune—and then give it to those ignorant, bloodsucking Kittredges into the bargain? Of all the stupid, harebrained—"

"Valerian!" Allegra interrupted, putting her gloved fingers against his lips to stifle his protests. "You have not brought me to England in vain. You saved me from Bernardo, for one thing. And you have given me back my family, after I thought myself to be all alone in the world. If I live to be one hundred I cannot thank you enough for what you have done."

"If you mean to put me to the blush, imp, you are fair and far out," Valerian told her, speaking around her fingers. "From what I've heard, I've done nothing more than land you in a nest of vultures who wish to strip you of your name while dressing you up like a dowager in mourning."

Allegra laughed. "*Nonno* is not the soft, cozy grandfather I could have wished for, I will admit that easily, but he is at heart a fine, if shallow, man. The Kittredges, for good or ill, are the only other family I have—and the most *sorry*—looking trio I have ever seen. But they are also totally useless to themselves, I think, and it is not their fault that I was born. How can you believe I should sleep nights if I allowed *Nonno*'s plan to make friends with the good Saint Peter end with my *zia* and *Cugina* Isobel sleeping in the damp gutters of Brighton? *Cugino* Gideon, I must tell you," she added with a smile, "I do not find it so terribly easy to worry about."

Valerian hated to admit it, but the child made sense, bless her generous heart. He could feel all his anger fading away and raised a hand to hold her fingertips against his lips a moment longer. "It might help them build character," he then suggested with a wry smile, trying to picture Gideon Kittredge camping in a gutter.

Allegra drew back her hand, doing her best not to pay attention to the way her fingertips now tingled in such a delicious manner. "You won't tell my *nonno*, will you, Valerian? It makes him so happy to think he is making his sister's life a misery."

Valerian's left eyebrow rose a fraction. "And that doesn't bother you?"

"No. Should it? *Zia* Agnes is not a nice woman. It does not hurt me to see her suffer for a while when I know she will come out right at the end. Besides, as long as she believes she will lose all *Nonno*'s money when he dies, she will take very good care to keep him most happily alive. And, before you ask me, I do not feel the least bit naughty spending *Nonno*'s money for him now—money that should have been my *madre*'s—great heaps of money—while he is able to see where it goes. *Capisci?* Understand? I still think I must get my sometimes terrible temper from my dear *papà*, but if I am mean, it only proves my Dugdale blood."

Valerian helped her to her feet. "And whom do we blame, imp, for your twisted logic? No, don't bother to answer, for I think I know. You are a woman. That is answer enough. Now, even if you are not cold, I am—as well as dizzy from listening to the way your mind works. I suggest we return to your grandfather's house before you tell me anything else and I slide into a sad decline.''

She slipped her hand once more around his forearm and allowed herself to be led back the way they had come. "*Uncail* Max warned me that you were a difficult man," she said, sighing. "Do you think, Valerian, that I am a difficult woman?"

"I think, imp, that you are a very generous child—although perhaps you are also still a little confused by all that has happened to you in the past weeks. I can only suggest that you give yourself some time before you make any binding decisions."

"Of course, of course," Allegra answered absently, pulling him toward a shop window. "Oh, Valerian, it is beautiful, is it not?" she asked, pointing to a gown hanging just behind the display in the bow window. "It's like *un romanzo rosa*—a pink novel. A perfect love story of a gown."

Valerian sighed and closed his eyes. Allegra might be different in many ways, but she was proving very much like all other women when it came to her wardrobe. He knew what would happen if he stepped inside this shop with her. He would be trapped for hours.

He felt her tug at his arm once more and sighed, knowing what he had to do. Reluctantly, he led Allegra into the shop.

Once inside, Valerian was in for a surprise as Allegra, upon being greeted by a thin, sallow-faced

Frenchwoman, immediately launched herself into a torrent of faultlessly accented French that left him standing with his mouth open. Within a matter of minutes Allegra had disappeared into a dressing room, the shopkeeper trotting behind holding gown, shoes, hose, cape, and elbow-length kid gloves.

It had taken Allegra only that long to make her selections, eyeing the contents of the shop from one end to the other with the sharp eye of one who knows exactly what she wants.

How different this was from Valerian's previous experiences in such places, when he had accompanied his mistress of the moment to Bond Street in the years before he'd learned that a simple gift of money was just as appreciated, if not more so. He had hated the experience then and he had believed he should hate the experience now, but so far Allegra was proving him wrong. Finding himself a seat in a corner, he sat down beside a vase filled with large feather plumes that insisted upon drooping onto his left shoulder, to await further developments.

He didn't have long to wait. After making him promise to "squeeze your eyes closed, ever so tightly, Valerian, and do not open them until I tell you," Allegra stepped out of the dressing room, the French-woman walking behind her, wringing her hands and weeping at the beauty of the sight in front of her.

"All right, Valerian." Allegra spoke from somewhere in front of him. "I will allow you to open your eyes now."

He obeyed, not realizing that his world was about to change forever.

Valerian, at the age of two and twenty, had taken a fall from his favorite horse, landing flat on his back so that all of his wind had been knocked out of him. He hadn't been able to curse, or to yell, or even to breathe. He had only been able to lie there, not really hurt, but just looking up at his mount, disbelieving that the animal could have surprised him so.

He felt the same way now. Unable to talk. Unable to think. Unable to breathe. Able only to look.

The gown Allegra wore had been fashioned of the richest taffeta and was white without really being white, but more like a deep, rich cream. The body of the gown was magnificently simple, hugging her tightly just beneath the breasts, then sweeping downward to a simple hem adorned only by a modest edging of taffeta flower petals sewn with tiny seed pearls.

The entire bodice, what there was of it, and to Valerian's mind there was precious little, was similarly decorated, each of them at least one hundred separate, pearled petals so cunningly placed on both the bodice and the short, off-the-shoulder puffed sleeves that Allegra's shoulders and head seemed to rise from the gown like a perfect summer rose in full bloom.

Her breasts were not overly exposed, but only gently hinted at, the slight cleavage revealed by the cut of the bodice rendering the illusion of enticing innocence rather than deliberate enticement. With every breath she took, the pearled petals trembled delicately, subtly, causing Valerian's blood to pound heavily against the base of his throat.

Allegra's naturally pink lips and cheeks, sparkling sapphire eyes, and deep-as-midnight curls gave the only real color to what, to his bemused mind, could only seem to be a painting of some glorious angel come to Earth.

Was this the same dusty termagant he had discovered in Florence—the barefoot urchin with a string of garlic sausages stuffed in her bodice? Could this glorious creature possibly be the same child he had teased about her voracious appetite, or been ashamed to be seen with in public, or even the one he had dismissed as a child who—although intriguing—was not really a woman, and most definitely not the woman for him?

Valerian fought the sudden urge to flee for his life.

"Well—are you going to say something or are you just going to stand there? What do you think? I am a thing of beauty, yes?" Allegra took hold of the skirt on either side and made a half-turn, looking back over her shoulder at him. "Madame Mathieu says she has poured her life into this gown but there has never been anyone she wished to sell it to—until now. I do so love to be in costume, and this is just like a costume, isn't it? Oh, that I might ever appear on stage in such a magnificent creation! I should then be the real prima donna!"

Allegra turned back to her still mute audience of one, frowning. "Valerian, you are once more looking at me in that strange way. Say something quickly, please, for you are beginning to make me nervous, and I do not like it."

Valerian rose, not without effort, unable to stop staring at Allegra's animated face. "She—" He had to stop and clear his throat. "She'll take it. What else do you have, madame?"

AGNES KITTREDGE, of course, had been appalled. First of all, no real lady frequented a dress shop with a man. What were people to think? Only kept women did such things. Thankfully it had only been that strange little "Madame Matthew's" shop, where no one of any importance would even think of making a purchase, yet alone browse, so perhaps they could scrape by without a major scandal.

Next there was the price! Ships had been launched for less. Armies had been fed for less. For Allegra had not stopped at that single gown, or the accessories so necessary to set it off. Oh, no. With that bewitched Valerian Fitzhugh's help, she had all but bought out the shop, blithely sending the bill to her grandfather.

Her grandfather—ha! To Agnes, this perhaps was the unkindest cut of all. The insolent chit didn't even know how to spell the man's name. Agnes knew, for Agnes had peeked at the bill when the mountain of striped boxes had been delivered—with even more to be delivered in the next few weeks.

"To be paid for by the Baron Dennis Dugdale*o*," Allegra had scribbled across the bottom of the bill in a bold, almost masculine script. The chit had put an O on the end of the reverend Dugdale name, just as if Denny were Italian! Why, it was almost enough to make a grown woman—a grown woman who had not herself seen a new gown in nearly three months—weep.

It *was* enough to make a young woman weep,

which was precisely what Isobel did when she, while Allegra and Betty were out on yet another of their lengthy walks, sneaked into her cousin's bedchamber and took a peek into the armoire.

Pinks, yellows, greens, whites, lavenders, and robin's egg blues. Silks, velvets, taffetas, bastistes, percales, and muslins. Morning gowns, redingotes, tunics, spencers, and shawls. Even a cashmere *canezou,* or hussar vest, edged with bands of sable. There was so much it threatened to spill from the armoire in a pastel rainbow of colors.

But that was not all. To supplement the fine but fairly meager wardrobe she had brought with her from Italy, Allegra now also had drawer after drawer filled with the finest linen handkerchiefs, kid gloves, silk stockings, lace-trimmed petticoats, chemises—and not a single corset.

There were three embroidered silk purses, five pairs of silk slippers, a pair of overshoes, a multitude of combs and artificial flowers to be worn in the hair, two ivory fans, and three bonnets—any one of which Isobel would have gladly died for, not that she would ever tell her cousin that.

The worst, the very worst of it all, was that there existed nothing in the armoire or the drawers that even vaguely suited Allegra. Didn't Valerian know that, even if her silly half-foreign cousin was too blinded to see it?

Allegra should never have been encouraged to buy such pale, flowery shades or such close-fitting styles. Her disturbing physical "faults" needed to be subdued, not accented. Egyptian earth. Pea green. Tobacco brown. And whiter-than-white whites. Those were the colors Isobel would have chosen for Allegra. And high necks. And lots and lots of lace. Yes, definitely a multitude of lace, to hide the girl's "embarrassing" figure.

She told her mother as much, unfortunately while Gideon was in the room, so that the startled young man found himself forced to submit to a half-dozen sharp slaps between his shoulder blades from his frantic mama in order to relieve himself of the bite of muffin that had, thanks to his nearly hysterical laughter, become wedged in his throat.

This did not make for a reconciliation of brother and sister after a lifetime of spats, which otherwise might have transpired, considering the fact that they both had so much to lose if Allegra were truly to be named the Baron's heir. It also did not endear Isobel to her mother, who had, just for a few single heart-stopping moments, believed she was about to see her beloved Gideon turn purple and expire, right in her lap.

"Mama, Uncle Denny doesn't seem to care a whit that Allegra is spending his money as if he is already belowground," Isobel added once her brother had finished wiping his streaming eyes and again taken up his familiar stance in front of the mantelpiece, totally neglecting to mention that the crime with which she had just accused Allegra could also most easily be laid at the collective Kittredge feet. "We have to do something quickly, Mama, before she spends his last groat!"

"Or marries Valerian Fitzhugh," Gideon slid in

neatly, so that Agnes was forced to cough discreetly into her handkerchief at her adored son's great wit.

"Mama!" Isobel cried, pushing at her mother's shoulder. "Make him stop!" She turned to her brother. "You're horrid, Gideon. Perfectly horrid." Her eyes narrowing, she attacked in her turn. "How long are you going to hide out behind Mama's skirts like some cringing coward, avoiding your creditors? That's why you're haunting the house, isn't it, instead of running the streets with your ramshackle gambling friends? Because you don't dare stick your nose outside for fear someone will break it for you?"

"That will be enough, Isobel!" Agnes unceremoniously pushed her daughter back against the settee cushions, putting an end to this distasteful exchange. "I should have known better than to think that Isobel could put aside her petty jealousies to help us, Gideon," she said, rising to go to her son. "But you, my darling, are not so foolish, are you?"

Gideon, who was indeed that foolish and did not have the faintest idea what the woman was talking about, placed a kiss on his mother's cheek and murmured, "Ah, Mama, you know me so well."

Isobel sighed, giving up the fight as she always did, for she was intelligent enough to know that after a lifetime of losing every battle to her brother, she was not about to win this one. "You don't seem to be completely cast down by Allegra's latest mischief, Mama. Do you, perhaps, have some sort of plan to rid us of her?"

Agnes walked to the doorway, looked both ways into the hall, then shut the door and locked it. "I do have a plan, my children,'' she all but whispered, ''and it will benefit both of you—all of us—although it will take some personal sacrifice on Gideon's part.''

Gideon stood up very straight, ''*Me,* Mama?'' he said, incredulous. Why, he had never been asked to do anything personally sacrificing in his life—except maybe that time, at the age of twelve, when he had been forced by his mama to write a thank-you message to his paternal grandmother for giving him, upon that man's death, his late grandfather's pearl stickpin. He stuck out his bottom lip, instantly turning mulish. ''What must I do *now?*''

Agnes Kittredge threw back her thin shoulders and lifted her head, the movement remotely possible of convincing any onlooker that she did indeed possess a chin. ''It is quite simple, actually. Isobel will have a free run at Fitzhugh—although why she should think he wants her remains a mystery to me—we shall have our fortune back, and Gideon, you shall have all the blunt you need at your fingertips. All you have to do, distasteful as this may be to you personally, is to *wed* Allegra Crispino!''

Isobel gave a small shriek, pressing her hands to her mouth. ''It is a glorious idea, Mama! But wait—that would mean that Allegra would still live under this roof. I do not think I should like that, for she is not the most temperate person, and seems to actually enjoy flying into rages.''

But Agnes wasn't listening. She was concentrating on the expression that had stolen, unbidden, onto her beloved son's face, a look that could only be termed ''lascivious.'' It was so difficult to believe, so crushing to learn that her son, her adorable little boy, could possibly be susceptible to carnal urges.

"Gideon!" she exclaimed, tottering to a nearby chair, as she was feeling decidedly faint. "Show some respect! You are in the presence of your mother!"

IT WAS THURSDAY AT LAST, and Allegra was rapidly becoming a bundle of nerves, just as she did before every important performance.

She had spent an hour that morning simply standing outside the Marine Pavilion, imagining herself as she would look sitting beneath the great chandelier in the Banqueting Room, or walking, arm in arm with the Regent himself, through the Long Corridor, and then—would her heart never stop its fearful pounding that made it feel as if it would burst?—standing directly beneath the vast dome of the Music Room as she gifted her host with an aria from the great Alessandro Scarlatti, father of the modern opera.

"Or perhaps I should do something lighter, something from Rossini's *Il Barbiere di Siviglia*," Allegra mused aloud as Betty tucked a single soft ivory silk rose into the mass of curls that had been combed through so carefully and then heaped atop Allegra's head. She looked up at the maid. "I do that very well, you know."

Betty turned her mistress's face back toward the mirror. "I'm sure you do, missy, iffen it's anything like what you was singing earlier in your tub. That was proper wonderful. I had to shoo two of those nosy footmen from your door, they were listening so hard.

Was that song from this *Sivi—Sigl*—oh, you know what I mean.''

Allegra smiled at her reflection, liking the dramatic touch the rose, set just behind her ear, had given her. So she'd had an audience, had she? It was good to know that her voice had not become too rusty. ''It is called, in English, *The Barber of Seville*. The work is a comedy, you see, and very new, first performed less than two years ago in Roma. My *papà* always said comedy is my *trionfo*—my triumph. And yes, the song I sang in my tub was from that opera.''

Happy to have an audience, and hoping to rid herself of some of her nervousness, Allegra proceeded to hum some of the first aria, only to be interrupted by a loud knocking on the door to her bedchamber.

''There you are, gel!'' Baron Dugdale bellowed, barging into the room without waiting for an answer to his knock. He walked slowly—as his immense bulk would have had him do even if it were not for his bandaged foot and unwieldly, gold-topped cane—carrying a large flat velvet box in his right hand.

''Here,'' he said, pushing the box at Allegra, who had stood up, smoothing the front of her ivory gown. ''These belonged to your grandmother. It's only fitting, I guess, that you should have them. And there's plenty more where these came from, only pearls is for purity, you know. Yes, your grandmother always told me Mary should wear the pearls first.''

Allegra looked at the jewelry box, knowing whatever lay inside it should have graced her *madre*'s neck, and hesitated.

''What? Are you waiting for me to tell you how

beautiful you look, eh? Well, you do, you know. Pretty as a picture. I shall have to use my cane here to beat the men away from you. Now, put these on. I don't want to be late.''

"Yes, *Nonno*," she responded quickly, shaking off her momentary melancholy. She took the box and gingerly opened it, as if a snake might have taken up residence atop the satin bed within. Then, all restraint flown, she gasped, "Oh, *Nonno*, they're beautiful!''

Betty helped Allegra put the heavy old-fashioned gold-and-pearl earrings in her ears, then lifted the waist-length double strands of lightest pink pearls over her head.

Allegra turned back to the mirror, her hands going to the pearl ropes as they skimmed over her bare skin and lay lightly against the ivory flower petals. Then she touched the tips of the earrings that cascaded from her ears like miniature waterfalls.

Tears stung at her eyes as she saw her grandfather's reflection in the mirror, his face nearly puce with what had to be pride. She whirled about and stood up on tiptoe, giving him a resounding kiss on each cheek.

"Yes, well—" he blustered, pushing her away. "Are we ready to go now, or are you going to stand there preening all the night long?''

Taking his arm, Allegra asked, "Is *Zia* Agnes ready, *Nonno?* I have not seen her all of the afternoon, or Isobel.''

"Aggie?'' The Baron threw back his head and laughed. "She's not invited. Nor that die-away daughter of hers either. Whatever could you be thinking, gel? Prinny don't like prickly weeds cluttering up his beautiful Pavilion.''

They made their way slowly down the stairs, a footman at the Baron's left side to add his support as they went. ''Took Aggie the once you understand, but it didn't work out. She complained the whole night long.'' He pulled a face and mimicked his sister in a high, singsong voice. '' 'It's too hot. There is too much food, too many dishes. The singing is too loud, the ladies' dresses too low. The music is too hearty.' Odds fish! I'd rather ride bareback on a greased pig than live through another night like that! The woman has no appreciation!''

Betty, who had run on ahead, met Allegra at the bottom of the stairs with the pink-lined ivory cape that matched Allegra's gown, its neck a wide ruff of pearl-studded flower petals.

''Oh, dear, I didn't know,'' Allegra responded, trying to appear downcast after her grandfather had given her what, to her, was the most exciting news of the evening: she would not have to feel *Zia* Agnes's frowns following her everywhere she went. ''Well, I promise not to complain about the amount of food the Regent serves. I can hardly wait, and have purposely starved myself all day in anticipation.''

''Meaning, I should imagine, that you carefully limited yourself to no more than two desserts at luncheon. How very brave of you, imp.''

''Valerian!'' Allegra whirled about to see Fitzhugh standing at the entrance to the small drawing room, her heart pounding even more furiously than it had when she thought of performing for the next King of

England. "You didn't tell me you too have been invited to the Marine Pavilion. You are going, aren't you? You look entirely too magnificent for just an ordinary evening."

It was true. Valerian had dressed himself very carefully, daring to wear formal evening clothes made expressly for him during his time in Paris. His black velvet breeches fit him like a second skin. The matching single-breasted, split-tailed coat, piped and lined in the finest white satin, was left open over a form-fitting black waistcoat, the white silk being repeated inside the tails of the coat, at his lace-ledged cuffs, and in the formally tied neckcloth and frills that peeped above the shawl collar of yet a second, white satin waistcoat.

White silk stockings and black leather pumps completed the outfit, as he could not bring himself to wear the remainder of the French Restoration *ensemble,* which consisted of a sword hung from a special belt, limiting himself to his usual restrained jewelry. He did, however, carry a black ostrich-fringed felt bicorne under his arm, knowing the hat to be *de rigueur.*

He had left his estate an hour previously, confident he looked his best, but now, with Allegra walking fully around him, her eyes wide in awe, he silently wished he had remembered the name of his French tailor so that he might send the man a gift.

He had given a brief consideration to turning down the Prince Regent's invitation to what was known far and wide to be an interminable evening at the Pavilion—but it had been only a very brief consideration.

Allegra was to be present. Allegra, dressed in that beautiful gown, smiling that heartbreaking smile. Allegra, so alive, so vital, and doubtless to be the cynosure of all male eyes. Allegra, who would be the recipient of a dozen compliments—and two dozen invitations to go riding, driving, or otherwise engage in some other pursuit meant to allow a man some time alone with a comely young woman. Would he go to the Pavilion? A herd of Hannibal's war elephants couldn't keep him away!

"Do I pass inspection, imp?" Valerian asked once she had rejoined her grandfather.

"Oh, Valerian—you, you—" Allegra threw up her arms, unable to find words to explain just how wonderful he looked. "Do you know how nice your angel wings look when you wear black?"

"Angel wings? I have been likened to many things, imp, but never anything remotely heavenly."

"No, no. I mean only the bits of white hair among the black above your ears. I think of them as angel wings."

Valerian's spirits plummeted, for Allegra had just unwittingly reminded him of the more-than-fifteen-year difference in their ages. It was strange, but when he was with Allegra he did not usually feel the least bit old.

"We all are as imposing as the richest box holders at the *Teatro alla Scala*," she went on, heedless of Valerian's pain. "*Nonno*, don't you think Valerian is magnificent? You should wear two waistcoats, *Nonno*—if only to make it easier to catch more of the little drips when you eat."

The Baron, who had been noticeably quiet throughout this exchange, stepped forward, his eyes narrowed. "I didn't know you was invited, Fitzhugh. You ain't exactly one of our set, you know. Prinny don't usually invite young pups."

Valerian smiled, his good spirits restored. "That's true enough, Duggy. I may not be as young as Allegra, but I don't as yet have one foot in the grave either, do I? But no matter. It seems our dear Regent has heard of my extensive travels and wishes for me to regale him with stories of my adventures. I understand, in fact, that I am to sit at his right hand tonight, beside Lady Hertford, of course."

"Eh? Is that so? Well, I suppose that's all right, then," the Baron said as a footman jumped about, struggling to throw a cape over the man's bulk. "Shall we be off, then? I assume we will be taking your carriage, Fitzhugh?"

"Would you have it any other way, Duggy?" Valerian answered, holding out his arm to Allegra. "My dear? Shall we go?"

CHAPTER SEVEN

THE MARINE PAVILION was everything Allegra had hoped it would be, and more. Much more. Perhaps, as the hours spent at the heavily laden dining table ground on and the gas chandeliers above their heads hissed out light and enthusiasm-wilting heat, *too* much more, even for her.

Seated as she was, between her constantly chattering grandfather, who seemed to be in his element here, and an aging peer whose only claim to celebrity had been the dizzying speed with which he had run through a fortune it had taken his family six generations to amass, Allegra could not even see Valerian, much less hear a word of the lively conversation going on between him and the Regent.

Perhaps that was why she had unconsciously eaten so heartily of *les filets de volaille à la marcchale,* forgetting to heed Valerian's hastily whispered warning as he left her to go to his assigned seat that she should be careful not to partake overmuch from any one course, as another dozen equally appealing courses were sure to follow.

What seemed to be—and in reality was—several hours later, after having to wave away the tempting *les gâteaux glacés au abricots,* a truly heartbreaking denial, she forced herself to sample *les truffes à l'italienne,* if only to judge for herself the authenticy of the chef's claim. Truffles, she soon found to her delight, did survive translation.

When it came time to leave the Banqueting Room—a departure was announced none too soon, Allegra mused, deciding that the temperature in the room now missed exceeding that of Hades by no more than a single degree—she was quick to seek out Valerian and ask his opinion of the meal.

"There was a meal?" he quipped, discreetly wiping his forehead with an handkerchief pulled from his pants pocket. Obviously, in this heat, the black velvet, no matter how flattering, had been a mistake.

"Prinny kept me talking for so long that I must have missed it. The man is insatiable, Allegra. If it weren't for his duties and the war, I should imagine he would have spent his entire life tramping from country to country just to see the sights. You know, Allegra, it had never before occurred to me that a man such as our Prince Regent, a man who has so much, could in some ways be so deprived."

Allegra smiled sympathetically as they followed the rest of the company of nearly a hundred over-dressed guests down the hallway and toward the Music Room. "I had sensed that the Prince is not very popular in England, Valerian, but you sound as if you almost like him."

"I do, imp, don't I? But mostly I feel sorry for him. He lives in a dream world now, all alone, and I doubt that even he can sometimes distinguish between what is real and what is not. Do you know, he as much as told me tonight that he had been at Waterloo with Wellington, distinguishing himself in battle against Napoleon.''

Allegra frowned, failing to understand the significance of what Valerian had just said. ''And he was not? I thought all princes and kings were great soldiers. They are in operas.''

Valerian directed Allegra to the sight of the bulky Prince Regent, who had chosen to leave off his stays after his daughter's death, as two footmen helped lower the man into a chair.

''Not our Prince, Allegra. Until a few years ago, Prinny needed a winch to hoist him onto a horse. Now, well, now he doesn't even try. A great soldier? I think he will most probably go down in history more as a great spender of his subjects' money. I earlier heard someone say that the main chandelier alone in the Banqueting Room cost over five thousand pounds. If I sound bitter, Allegra, it is only because the real veterans of Waterloo, like Tweed, my coachman, have not fared half so well.''

Allegra recalled Tweed, and the black patch the man wore over the place where, before he had gone to war, his right eye had allowed him to look at the world through two eyes. ''I suppose that is true, Valerian. War is a terrible thing. But the chandelier is a pretty thing, Valerian, and I think the world sometimes needs pretty things as well, even more than it can know.''

''There are moments, imp,'' Valerian said softly, squeezing her gloved hand, ''when you make me feel a complete fool.''

Allegra felt much depressed as Valerian withdrew his hand, and she began looking about the enormous room in hopes of finding something that would lighten her spirits, something of which her companion did not know the price. It didn't take her long to discover that there existed not a single thing within the Music Room that failed to please her.

Her spirits soared, so that she felt more as she had done when first they had arrived at the Pavilion—before *les filets de volaille à la marcchale* and Valerian's sad stories about the Regent.

She truly did not know where to look first—at the strange pillars with bronze serpents coiling down them headfirst, at the exotic red Chinese laquered panels, or at the ribbon-wound bamboo side ceilings that were topped by an immense central dome made up of first blue, then gold scales, as if it mimicked the protective skin of some elegantly painted reptile.

There were chandeliers everywhere, lighting the room as if it were still daylight and showing off the strange gilt furniture that seemed to encourage people to lie half reclined rather than sit. But of premier importance to Allegra was the orchestra of at least seventy musicians who sat on one side of the room, their instruments at the ready.

"*Magnifico. Molto magnifico!* It is just like a great cathedral, Valerian, only pretty—and maybe just a tiny bit naughty," she declared fervently, which encouraged Valerian to laugh out loud.

Yes, everything in the Music Room pleased her, except perhaps a few of its occupants who seemed to be a little the worse for drink and prone to make disparaging remarks about their host, who had yet to join them. She couldn't help noticing the looks she was receiving from many of the gentlemen present— looks not difficult to interpret—nor did she really like the way the ladies seemed to ignore her in droves. Only one, a rather faded redheaded lady dressed in purple, had actually spoken to her at dinner, and then only to demand imperiously that she reveal the name of her dressmaker.

As he caught sight of a twice-widowed Marquis making his way in their direction, all but smacking his lips as he eyed Allegra's bodice, Valerian led the girl, who was still gazing upward in rapture at the immense dome, to a pair of blue brocade satin chairs at one side of the room. They sat down, only to rise again as the Regent entered, a heavily painted and ostrich-plume-topped Lady Hertford on his arm.

For the next two hours the Regent performed for his guests, playing the cello and then singing "Mighty Conqueror" and "Glorious Apollo" for them in a surprisingly pleasing baritone before commanding the assembled musicians to play—as he beat a hearty accompaniment on his knee—a nearly endless selection of his favorite musical works with, to Allegra's mingled delight and dismay, a most telling emphasis on Italian rococo.

It had passed eleven before Allegra, who had found herself growing weary in the overheated room, noticed that many of the guests were taking their leave, and made to follow them.

Valerian held her back. "No, imp, you aren't rescued yet. Duggy told me we are to be a part of the select few who have been honored with an invitation to retire with the Regent to a nearby drawing room for a cold supper.''

"Supper?" Allegra clapped a hand to her mouth as her exclamation seemed to echo in the rapidly emptying room. "Valerian, you can't be serious! I couldn't possibly eat a thing!"

"There you are, gel!" Baron Dugdale approached slowly, favoring his bandaged foot. "Good news, m'dear. I told Prinny all about your singing and he has agreed to hear you after supper. You singing, Lady Brownley playing at the harp—Lord help us— and the Earl of Somewhere-or-another is going to scrape away at a violin or some such nonsense."

He leaned forward, peering intently into her eyes. "You weren't funning me, gel, were you? Poor fellow seemed so pleased to hear he had a real *I*-talian here to sing for him, though for the life of me I don't know why. He just had some other foreign warbler here last month. They sing in their own lingo, you know, so that you can't understand a word of it even if you was to try, which I surely don't. Seems a waste of time to even listen to 'em, don't it? Well, never mind that. You'd best be good. It isn't smart to get on the wrong side of the next King of England."

Allegra had relaxed, having given up all hope of performing that night, but now her nervousness was back in double force, not that she would allow her grandfather to see it. "*Nonno,* I once sang for the Bishop of Bologna," she announced, her head thrown back challengingly. "I do not believe I should be an embarrassment to you—that is, *if* I should choose to sing tonight.''

Valerian thought for a moment that Lord Dugdale was going to reach out and slap his granddaughter. ''*If* you should choose to sing tonight? *If!*'' He turned to Valerian. ''Fitzhugh, what is the gel talking about? What does she mean—*if* she should choose to sing tonight?''

''*Hai messo il carro davanti ai buoi, Nonno.* You have put the cart before the oxen,'' Allegra retorted hotly, stepping directly in front of her grandfather so that he would stop looking to Valerian for answers that should be coming from *her* mouth.

Lord Dugdale employed the bottom third of his cane to push his granddaughter to one side, then all but bellowed at Valerian, ''What's she talking about, I asked you? Didn't she talk about singing here? Isn't that all she talked about in the carriage on our way? Besides, I ain't asking her to sing! Odds fish—I'm *telling* her!''

Allegra stepped in front of Dugdale yet again. It was true. She was dying to sing for the Regent, and had been longing even more to perform for him ever since hearing the most wonderful acoustics of the domed Music Room. But some things were more important than her deathly desires.

''Ah, *Nonno,* now you have hit the nail with the mallet! I am a great artist. It is just like I told my manager, that thickheaded Erberto. It is *I*, and I alone, who must be allowed to choose the time and place of my performances. And I do not think I choose to perform alongside what are sure to be hapless harp ladies and violin-destroying Earls.''

Valerian stuck his head past Allegra's shoulder and addressed the Baron. "Perhaps, Duggy, if Allegra and I might have a few moments alone?" he asked, hoping that for once in his life the older man would show some intelligence.

"Alone?" the Baron repeated, frowning. "I don't know, Fitzhugh." Then he brightened. "Odds fish, I guess it ain't like the two of you haven't been alone plenty before this, eh? In many ways you're almost sort of her guardian."

"Thank you so much, Duggy," Valerian responded, the other man oblivious to the fact that he most sincerely wanted to throttle him.

The Baron looked about to see that nearly everyone else had either departed for the evening or proceeded to the supper room. "Now I'm in for it! Prinny's already at table. Look, Fitzhugh—Valerian—be a good lad and talk some sense into this gel here, won't you? I suggest the small salon down the hall. Everyone uses it when they want to—well, never mind about that. You just make sure this gel sings!"

"POOR *NONNO*." Allegra collapsed, giggling deliciously, onto a striped satin settee in the discreetly placed salon. "I most probably should not have done that, but he must learn that I am not someone to be ordered about. I am a singer!"

"You sang mostly in the chorus, if memory serves," Valerian reminded her, sitting beside her after closing the door to the salon. "Now tell me, what are you going to perform for the Prince?"

Allegra sat forward, frowning. "He has dismissed the orchestra, you know. Oh, yes, I saw that most distinctly. They will not be back." She then rattled off a long stream of possible selections, holding each out verbally for inspection before, one by one, eliminating them all. She leaned against the back of the settee, which somehow was now draped most comfortably with Valerian's black velvet sleeve. "Oh, I do not know what I shall do."

Valerian looked down at her, seeing the adorable pout that had appeared on her enticingly pink lips, and swallowed hard.

He had to retain the knowledge that she was little more than a child.

He had to remind himself that he was a man of the world, an honorable man, and knew better than to steal a kiss from an innocent girl.

He had to remember that he, although so much older than she, and the possessor of angel wings, was still a reasonably young man of five and thirty, and not nearly ready to settle down and start his nursery.

He had to keep it clear in his mind that—"Oh, the hell with it!"

Valerian quickly shifted himself on the settee so that he sat slightly forward, turned in Allegra's direction, and took her chin between his fingers, "Imp," he said, his voice husky, "if you think I'm going to ask your permission for this first, you're fair and far out!" So saying, he lowered his head to hers and allowed himself to succumb to the sanity-destroying attraction of her moist, pouting mouth.

Allegra did not resist him, but rather welcomed him to her, winding her arms around his neck as he dared to deepen the kiss. He sensed rather than knew that this was her first kiss, for her reactions, although enthusiastic and wonderfully cooperative, were not at all practiced.

He could feel her body trembling under his hands and imagined that the hundreds of pearled petals were all rustling in a sweet summer breeze off the ocean. He could feel his own body begin to tremble as the passion Allegra's innocent seduction wove around him penetrated to the very heart of his being.

If he didn't stop soon, if he didn't remember who he was and where he was and what he was about to do, he would be hopelessly lost, caught forever in Allegra's magical spell. He should draw back. He should break off the kiss, apologize for his boorish behavior, get them both out of this exotic, tempting salon made for dalliance, and return Allegra to her grandfather.

He should. But he wouldn't. Not when he lifted his head a fraction, opened his eyes, and saw the blissful, rapturous expression on Allegra's beautiful face. He couldn't. If all of Prinny's dragons chose that moment to come to life and breathe their hottest fires or if all the bronze snakes began to hiss his name, Valerian could not have broken away from her.

Taking hold of her bare shoulders, he crushed her to him once more.

"Now, and isn't this a most lovely picture, don't

you know? The toadeating old man is in the supper room, none the wiser, chatting up Old Swellfoot. And while the cat's away, I always say, the mice will dance. Is that how it goes, my boyo?''

Valerian broke from Allegra so quickly that he nearly toppled backward onto the floor. ''Max!'' He couldn't believe it. Maximilien Murphy in Brighton? In the Marine Pavilion? Why? How? He turned to see a short, pudgy man dressed in the formal wear and powdered wig of Prinny's Banqueting Room servants. ''What are you doing here?''

''Yes, it is I, Maximilien P. Murphy, at your service.'' Max made his stunned audience a most magnificent leg (considering the tightness of his breeches), closed the door, and walked across the room to kiss Allegra on both cheeks. ''What am I doing here? Up to a few minutes ago I was helpin' to clear up the mess you people made over dinner, if you must hear it. Coulda fed all Dublin and half of County Clare on the scraps, don't you know? Isn't this the place, though? I don't think I've ever seen such a mess of grandeur.''

''*Uncail* Max,'' Allegra said, hopping to her feet to throw her arms about his neck, ''it is so wonderful to see you again. Candie, and Tony, and the so-adorable Murphy—they are all fine?''

''Fine as shamrocks on a sunny day, child, though I'm wagering Candie wouldn't be so happy to see what's been going on in here. Then again, knowing my Candie, I must reconsider. She probably would be cock-a-hoop! Why, I remember her telling me how

Tony, that rascal, climbed in through her bedroom window and—''

''Never mind that,'' Valerian broke in hurriedly. ''Max, I repeat—what are you doing here? Here in Brighton, and most especially here in the Pavilion? I thought you were living in Italy because you're a wanted man in England.''

''Well, and of course I am, my boyo. And why d'you think I'm wearing this blasted, itchy wig?'' He turned to Allegra. ''You shouldn't be letting him kiss you, don't you know. Lovemaking always did have the power to rattle a man's brains.''

Allegra blushed very prettily, and she did so now, murmuring, ''Yes, *Uncail* Max. I'm very sorry.''

''No, you're not,'' Murphy shot back at her, winking. ''Fib, m'darlin', for a good fib may take you anywhere, but never lie.''

Valerian crossed to the door, opened it, and looked out, to be sure the hallway was clear. ''Never mind that now, Max,'' he commanded, all his passion now fled, and his thoughts again directed to the happenings of the moment. ''What's wrong? It has to be something very important for you to take the chance of coming to the Pavilion.''

''It could be and it couldn't be.'' Max sat himself down beside Allegra on the settee and reached a hand into a nearby candy dish, popping a comfit into his mouth. ''But it can wait, boyo. Could you and the beautiful little colleen here meet me tomorrow on the Steine, say at two in the afternoon? You won't know me, so I'll find you. We'll make our plans then.''

As Max started for the door, Valerian grabbed his

arm, pulling him back. "This could have waited for tomorrow, couldn't it, Max? You only sneaked in here, right under Prinny's nose, for nothing more than the thrill of the thing, didn't you?"

The Irishman grinned from ear to ear. "Ah, boyo, you're an apt student of human nature. I like that in a man." He looked past Valerian to wag a finger in Allegra's direction. "And it's a good thing I came here tonight, I'm thinking. If it's designs on turning into a hoyden you have, m'girlie, you'd best think again. First the ring and the promise—then the kiss. Remember that, darlin'."

"Yes, *Uncail* Max," Allegra replied, her sapphire eyes dancing. "I'll be very sure to remember that." She looked toward Valerian, who was in his turn glaring at Max. "I always remember *everything*."

"IN BOCCA AL LUPO," Valerian whispered as Allegra rose from her chair, using an Italian saying meant to wish her good luck, but that sounded much better in Italian, as it translated to English only as "in the wolf's mouth."

He watched as she stepped to the exact center of the Music Room, curtsied deeply in the Regent's direction, and rose to stand facing the future King, her hands decorously folded at her waist.

Allegra was the last to perform, a condition she had laid down to her grandfather, saying that it wouldn't be fair to the other two performers to have to follow her lead. The occupants of the room, some of them more than half drunk and all of them yawning into their hands, could be heard squirming in their seats, eager for the interminable evening to come to an end.

Allegra waited until all sound had stopped, her chin high. The chandeliers threw a bright but flattering light, calling attention to her small, beautifully clad, regally erect frame.

Valerian thought he would burst with pride. He tore his gaze from her and sneaked a quick look around the room, smiling, he was sure, like a preening old hen with one chick. She held every occupant in the palm of her little hand, and she had yet to sing a note.

He could not know that, inside, Allegra was trembling so violently she thought she might become ill. He could not know that she would sing that night, not for the Regent, not for all the titled ladies and gentlemen, not even for her own enjoyment. Tonight she would sing for Valerian. Tonight she would give the performance of her life!

Just as Valerian was beginning to worry that Allegra might be hesitating too long, that she had become a victim of her own bravado and in truth could sing nary a note, she opened her mouth and, with the first pure, sweet sound that issued forth, dispelled his every fear.

She sang an aria from some Italian opera or other—Valerian did not readily recognize it or even care—her voice even more beautiful than she, if that were possible. The aria asked a lot from her—laughter, deep sorrow, amusement, elation, despair—and she gave herself over to the music most generously, her hand movements eloquent, her face animated, her eyes twin sapphire mirrors of deeply felt emotion.

Somehow—he would never afterward remember precisely when or how it had happened—he found himself standing, unable to remain seated in the presence of such beauty. He had always enjoyed attending the opera, in a social sort of way, but never had he been struck by anything as he was now by Allegra's effortlessly soaring voice. He knew, just as well as he knew his name, that the memory of this night would comfort him every time he looked into her eyes and, if she were ever to leave his side, haunt him unceasingly into his grave.

When it was over, the room remained silent, echoing only the last, long note of Allegra's musical story. She turned toward him, her expression questioning, just as Prinny leapt from his chair, clapping loudly and calling, *"Bravo! Bravo!"*

A heartbeat later the Music Room exploded into pandemonium. The previously sleepy, jaded audience came to life, rushing to follow its host's lead, each person trying to outdo the other with either praise or applause.

Valerian did not join them. He did not clap. He did not shout. He simply stood there, he and Allegra looking at each other as if no one else were in the room, until the crush of people eager to congratulate her took her from his sight.

"You've gone beyond hope, you know," Max Murphy said from somewhere behind him. "I've seen it all before, with Tony and my Candie, and I know all the signs."

Valerian didn't even bother to turn around. "I don't know what you're talking about, Max," he said, knowing that no one, least of all someone as astute as Maximilien P. Murphy, would ever believe him. "And shouldn't you be going before you're found out? Not to be nasty, Max, but you're not half so young or sleek as the rest of Prinny's servants, and you're beginning to stick out like a sore thumb."

"It's goin' I'll be doing now, boyo, until tomorrow at two," Max said, chuckling, clearly not taking offense at anything a silly, lovestruck soul should say to him. "But it's too late for you to be goin' anywhere, no matter what the time. Your heart, don't you know, has already flown."

ALLEGRA DANCED about her bedchamber, her arms held wide, unable to contain her ecstasy. She felt like a child who has just been granted its most favorite wish, unable to sit still, but forced by her own inner excitement to constantly remain on the move.

"Oh, Betty!" she exclaimed, grabbing onto one of the bedposts and leaning back, swinging herself lightly from side to side, dressed only in her chemise. "You cannot know, you cannot imagine it! I am the *sensazione!* The pudgy Prince, he adores me, he *weeps* in adoration! And, ah, Betty—my *nonno!* My *nonno* puffs and preens and so forgets himself as to rush into the multitude of supplicants crowding about me and allows some stupid person to step on his poor toe! And still he doesn't care. No! He tells everyone, 'This is *my* granddaughter, to whom I am giving a plum!' Betty, I cannot tell you how I enjoyed myself!"

The maid, who had spent the last hour chasing Allegra around the room in order to divest her of her gown, and who had been trying without success since then to get her mistress to bed, at last collapsed onto the mattress herself, saying, "Yes, missy, you *can* tell me. You have *been* telling me, over and over again. And if you don't stop gallopin' about the place singing little bits of that foreign stuff, you'll be telling the whole household!"

Allegra abandoned the bedpost to dance across the room and snatch a flower from a nearby arrangement. She sniffed of its delicate fragrance, then tucked its dripping stem into the top of her chemise as she looked at the drowsy maid. Betty, it would appear, was becoming bored. Well, Allegra would soon put an end to that! "Ah, you terrible grouchy person, I refuse to listen to you. But did I tell you of my assignation—I think that is the correct word—with Mister Valerian Fitzhugh in one of the small salons?"

"Your *what?*"

Allera hopped up onto the mattress, sitting on her knees. "Ah, I had thought not," she teased, grinning mischievously. "He kissed me, Betty," she whispered confidentially, leaning toward the bug-eyed maid. "He kissed me twice. He dragged me off to a private salon and we were all alone, just the two of us, in the beautiful Pavilion. It was most delightful! And I had not yet even sung for him!"

Betty rolled her eyes, sighing deeply. "Oh, laws, now what? Does your grandfather know?"

Allegra collapsed onto her back on the bed, her ebony tresses splayed out fanlike on the pillow, her fingers lightly stroking the deep pink flower petals lying against her breasts. "*Nonno?* No, he does not know. It is our secret, Betty. I wish to hug it to myself for a while longer. You do understand, don't you?"

Betty sniffed derisively, her common-sense mind far from clouded with rosy romantic images. "I understands it all right, missy. You've gone and compromised yourself good. And to think I always thought that Mister Fitzhugh fella to be a fine gentleman. He should be ashamed of himself!"

Allegra turned her head on the pillow, her eyes shining with mischief. "Oh, I think Valerian is very much ashamed with himself, Betty. I turned to him when my aria was done and caught him looking at me in that strange way I told you about, the one that makes my toes curl up in my slippers. That look used to worry me, but now I like it very much, as my toes curled up the same way tonight, when he kissed me."

Betty clapped her hands over her ears. "Please, missy, I don't think I want to hear any more about this kiss."

"Two kisses, Betty. Betty? Valerian barely had a word for me all the way home, except to tell me he will be coming by tomorrow to take me walking on the Steine. He will propose marriage to me then, yes?"

Betty made a great business of pulling the bed-clothes up over Allegra's slim body. "He'll be proposing somethin', missy. I've lived long enough to be sure of that! Now you'd best get to sleep or it will soon be time to get up." She walked to the door, blowing out candles as she went, only to turn back and say, "You know, missy, you shouldn't be in such a big hurry to wed. You'll have plenty of gentlemen to choose from before you're done. Why, I heard it below-stairs when I went down for tea that Master Gideon is planning to ask for your hand.''

''Gideon!'' Allegra sat up, her smile wide. ''Oh, yes, Betty, I can see Gideon now, down on one knee in front of me in the drawing room, begging to be allowed to make passionate love to my inheritance.'' She collapsed once more onto the pillows and gave way to another attack of the giggles. ''Gideon for my *nonno*'s fine fortune and, I am thinking, sad, silly Isobel for poor Valerian, whom she is so sure she loves. Oh, My. *Prendi due piccioni con una fava*, Betty. *Zia* Agnes, I think, wishes to catch two pigeons with one bean! Now I am even more impatient for tomorrow to arrive so that I can tell the other pigeon!''

VALERIAN'S DISPOSITION, as he continued pacing the length of his study two hours after arriving back at his estate just outside Pyecombe, was not quite so carefree as Allegra's.

His mind insisted upon spinning backward in time, trying in vain to discover just where it was that he had made a small turning in the road, leading himself unwittingly, unknowingly, into quite the most confusing, confounding, intriguing chapter of his life.

Had he sealed his fate the day he had opened the missive from Baron Dugdale enlisting his aid in locating his lordship's long-lost granddaughter? Or had he set the stage for his downfall only after agreeing to act as Good Samaritan for the Baron?

He swallowed the last of his fireside-warmed

brandy and ran a hand distractedly through his hair. Perhaps it had been the moment Allegra, barefoot, smelling of sausages, and clad in her soiled, peasant-like dress, had turned to him and announced quite clearly that she would not sleep with him.

He poured another snifter and rubbed the glass between his palms, warming it.

Failing that memorable moment in Florence, he knew he would always remember their departure from Naples and the way Allegra had cried so brokenheartedly against the front of his greatcoat, her slim arms wrapped tightly about his waist as if he were the only remaining solid thing in life that she had to cling to.

Or could he have taken the fatal step that first day in Brighton when, against his better judgment, he had remained at the Dugdale residence, impatiently awaiting Allegra's summons to her bedchamber, rather than following his inborn self-protective masculine instincts and taking to his heels just as fast as he could?

He took a deep sip of the brandy, grimacing as it burned the back of his throat. No, it had been none of those times. Yes, they all had something to do with his current pitiful condition, that he acknowledged, but none of them were the single, telling blow, the final determination that, for good or ill, he would never be the same man he had been before Allegra Crispino had come literally crashing into his heretofore neat, orderly life.

It was arriving home at his estate after first delivering Allegra to her grandfather that had done it for him, finally made him realize he had crossed the river to real love for the first time in his life and then, without ever once considering the danger, had proceeded to burn all his bridges behind him.

Everywhere he looked, in each room of his house, in his gardens, while riding across his budding fields, he had seen Allegra, envisioned how she would look if she were there, sharing each moment with him. Without her, without Valerian being able to see his surroundings the way she would see them, through eyes shining with innocent wonder, his whole world had turned to a lifeless gray, and he would not have been able to stay away from Brighton another moment, with or without the Baron's request that he attend him.

He sank into his favorite chair, smiling ruefully at the memory of that day.

The time spent with Allegra, hunting down elusive hothouse cherries for the Baron, walking and talking as they wove their way together through the streets of Brighton, had only served to prove once and for all that he, Valerian Fitzhugh, was a doomed man.

But he had still secretly held out hope that he could be wrong, that he was only suffering from a temporary delusion that had him dreaming wistfully of carefree days listening to Allegra's chatter while he feasted on her beauty, and of quiet nights spent in front of the fire, Allegra's dark head trustingly pressed against his shoulder.

And then there would be the travel, the places he would take her to just so that he could see them again through her eyes, and the children they would have, sapphire-eyed, dark-haired girls and little boys who had their father's features and their mother's unquenchable spirit...

"Damn it!" Valerian's fist came down on the arm of the chair, making a loud, smacking sound in the quiet room. He shouldn't have kissed her! No matter what his excuse, no matter how terrible the temptation, he should never have kissed her!

He threw back his head and laughed out loud at his own foolishness. He shouldn't have kissed her? No! He shouldn't have *stopped* kissing her! He should have kissed her, and held her, and loved her, until he was so lost, so completely at her mercy, that he would have dared there and then to ask this most delightful, beautiful creature to do him the supreme honor of becoming his wife.

But Max, blast his interfering Irish soul to Perdition, had put an end to all that.

Now it was too late. Now she had become the newest sensation in a society that lived for the next sensation. From this night on she would be fêted and pursued and fawned upon from the mighty on down. Now he would have to bide his time, allow her to bask in the full glow of her triumph at the Pavilion, and hope that she would deign to allow him some few small crumbs of her attention.

Only when she had been allowed to indulge herself in her newly found popularity, only after she had had her well-deserved Season as a Diamond of the First Water at the Assembly Rooms in Brighton and the ballrooms of London, only then could he in clear conscience dare ask her to become his wife.

He sat slumped in his favorite leather chair and

stared into the dying fire. Yes, that was what he would have to do now. He would have to play a waiting game. Unless, of course, he thought—rallying slightly as he remembered Max's appearance at the Pavilion—some other, less painful way was to present itself!

CHAPTER EIGHT

VALERIAN WAS going quietly out of his mind. It seemed as if he and Allegra could advance no more than three feet in any one direction before they were stopped by someone who wished to issue an invitation to her, speak to her, praise her, be seen with her.

As he smiled, and bowed, and tipped his hat, his eyes kept darting in every direction, endlessly searching for some sign of Maximilien Murphy, who was, by Valerian's pocket watch, a full twenty minutes late for their appointment.

Not that he seriously expected the wily Irishman to show his face in the midst of this crush. Was there no one left in London? Had every fool and his wife come to Brighton to be with the Prince? Valerian looked about him for a convenient side street down which, hopefully with Max watching, from some not-too-distant vantage point, he and Allegra might somehow escape this ridiculous crush of humanity.

Finally, just as Allegra was floundering badly in a rather one-sided conversation with Lady Bingham, who was imploring Allegra to attend a "small party in your honor on any evening of your choosing," Valerian mumbled some vague excuse, bowed to her ladyship, and all but pushed his companion around the corner and onto St. James's Street.

"You were rather rude, weren't you, Valerian?" Allegra questioned, tugging her arm free of his hold as they began walking down the nearly deserted street. "I have always much preferred someone to ask my permission before pulling me along as if I were no more than a sack of tomatoes on the way to market."

Valerian smiled down at her. "I stand corrected, imp. From now on I shall be sure to gain your agreement *before* I pull you along like a sack of tomatoes. Now, if you have done with accepting applause for your performance last night, perhaps I might drag your thoughts back to the project at hand?"

Allegra's full bottom lip jutted out as she made a great show of pouting before once more taking Valerian's arm and giving it a friendly squeeze. "I am very bad, am I not, Valerian? But I did so enjoy myself, with everyone complimenting me on my singing." She shook her head. "There were even flowers delivered from the Regent himself this morning. Did I tell you that? Yes, I suppose I did."

"Counting now, Allegra, you have told me four times," Valerian answered tightly, wishing he had had the presence of mind to send a bouquet himself.

"And to think I had worried that I should not be liked. I am very popular, yes?"

"I refuse to answer that, imp, or else your head might succeed in outgrowing that fetching bonnet. Now, did you see Max anywhere?"

Allegra instantly sobered, shaking her head. "I

looked for him, but I could not find him anywhere, and then there were all those people around us, so that I could not see anything. Oh, dear!'' she exclaimed, suddenly understanding. ''He could not dare to approach us while we were surrounded by all my new friends, could he? Valerian, do you think he has taken fright and gone away?''

''Max, frightened? Allegra, he dared to come inside the Pavilion last night, no doubt serving up vegetables to three dozen lords and ladies he had talked into parting with a good deal of their money at one time or another. My only concern right now is finding him so that we may discover what brought him to Brighton when he promised Candie he would stay in Italy.''

''He's got something boiling in the pot,'' Allegra declared, nodding. ''I think perhaps Max has heard of some trouble concerning me. Or else Erberto has returned, to give me back my wages, and Max has brought my money to me. Pooh! That cannot be it. Erberto would never do such a thing. Ah, but only to say his name is to see him!'' She began, alternately clapping her hands and pointing down the street. ''*L'uomo del giorno!* It is the man of the day! Isn't he wonderful?''

Valerian looked in the direction Allegra was pointing, frowned, then looked again. ''Max?'' he asked as a short, stout woman approached them, leaning heavily on a battered cane, her other arm encumbered by a wicker basket filled with small bouquets of rapidly wilting flowers. ''Good Lord, man, is it really you?''

''Violets! Violets! Who'll buy my sweet violets?''

Max called loudly, drowning out both Allegra's
delight and Valerian's question. He sidled up to them
and lowered his voice to a harsh whisper. "Of course
it is Max. Who was it you was expecting, boyo, the
Queen of the May? And, Allegra, much as you are
delighted by my presence, m'darlin', I would ask you
to stop kicking up such a devil of a wind about it,
please. I'd like to be seeing this day."

Valerian covered his mouth to stifle his laughter.
He could barely believe Max's peasant-woman appearance, and the gray wig that covered the man's
head could only be termed a master stroke. "Max,"
he said, grinning, "my compliments. You, as you
Irish say, make a fine doorful of a woman."

Max ignored this insult, turning to concentrate his
full attention on Allegra. "Quite the rising comet you
are, m'darlin'. Yes, it's watching you I've been, lug-
ging these posies about—made m'self a few pennies
doing it, by the by—and I'm here to warn you not to
take all this boot-licking to heart. The sheep only go
where Prinny leads 'em, and he'll be leading 'em
somewhere else before the cat can lick her ear, so you
keep that in mind and make the most of it for yourself
while you can."

"Ah, sage words of wisdom from the Bog Lander
in the petticoats. Allegra, mayhap you should embroider them on a pillow for your bed." Valerian
turned to Max, frowning. "What would you have the
imp do, Max, charge a fee for gracing their parlors
and end up in disgrace? Is that why you've come
here, to set yourself up as her new manager? Allegra's

singing career is over. She's an heiress now, and has no need of your help in that direction.''

Max lifted a bunch of violets and pressed them into Allegra's hands. "That'll be twopence, sir, and the lady thanks you very much," he said, holding out his upturned palm to Valerian for payment. "Didn't sleep well last night, did you, boyo? You're showing a mean streak I never saw before, don't you know?"

Valerian had the good grace to feel ashamed of himself and said as much to Max, adding, "It's just that I've been waiting all day for this meeting. What has happened that you felt the need to come to Brighton? Is Allegra in any danger?"

Max pocketed the coins, sneaking a look out of the corners of his eyes as if to make sure no one was close enough to overhear his next words. "It was bored I was, watchin' as Tony and my Candie billed and cooed, so I amused myself a bit by keepin' an eye on that Bernardo fellow. Besides, after sendin' m'dear Louisa—that's Miss Shackleford to you, Fitzhugh—along to chaperon Allegra, I thought I might just as well drop myself over here for a space and see how she's doin'."

"*Uncail* Max? You and Miss Shackleford are in love? I didn't know. Valerian, isn't that wonderful? Will there be a wedding?"

"Don't be daft, girlie. Max Murphy will never wed. My wife's intended mother died an old maid. No, it's a warning I've come to deliver to the both of you. The handsome shoemaker is on his way. Thanks to my generous Candie, I was able to take a faster ship, but he'll be here any time now, to claim his bride.''

"His bride? How could he continue to believe that I would ever—oh, no!'' Allegra rounded on Valerian, shaking the bouquet of violets in his face. "This is all your fault! You were the one who said I should wave to the fool as the ship left the dock. He probably thought I was sorry to leave him behind and wished for him to follow me. Oh! We are in a lovely pie now!''

"It would seem so. Persistent fellow, isn't he?'' Valerian mused, shaking his head, oblivious to Allegra's anger. He had wondered if Bernardo's impending arrival could be the problem Max had alluded to last night, but he hadn't been quite able to bring himself to believe the Italian's devotion would cause him to do anything so desperate. But then, he mused further, Allegra was a difficult woman to forget.

"Don't be beating on Valerian, m'darlin', for it's needing him again you'll be, I'll be thinking,'' Max interrupted just as Allegra looked about to deliver a punch to Fitzhugh's middle. "Bernardo comes alone, which evens up the odds a bit, but unless you wish to have the man serenading you outside your window at midnight, you'll have to find some way to convince the shoemaker you will never be his.''

Allegra, who had been feeling much abused, rallied. "You're right, Uncail Max. Valerian is a true ark of science—very smart. He will figure out just what we are to do. Something must be done. I cannot live my life with that foolish Timoteo forever chasing behind me like some hungry dog after a bone.''

Something was bothering Valerian. "Max, exactly how did Bernardo learn that Allegra was bound for Brighton?"

Murphy made himself very busy rearranging his remaining bouquets. "And what am I to be now, boyo, a mind reader? Unless I had a little slip of the tongue when I sat sipping wine with the lad in a local *caffè*, trying to discover what he planned."

He turned to Allegra. "It's on the water wagon I've been since the morning after you left, m'darlin', but I confess I took a most terrible tumble from it the day you and sweet Louisa sailed away—and you as well, Valerian. I'm that sorry, that I am, and not just because Candie read me one of her memorable scolds just while my head was pounding like to make me believe someone was doin' a jig behind my eyes."

"Oh, *Uncail* Max," Allegra all but groaned, shaking her head. "But I forgive you, for you must have been sorely tried to lose your Louisa. You forgive him as well, don't you, Valerian? Valerian?"

"Hmm?" Inspiration had struck Valerian with a force so hard he almost reeled under its onslaught, so that he hadn't really been listening. Could he do it? Would he be able to pull it off? And if he did do it, would it last? He looked at Max, his expression purposely blank. "I suppose—and this may be just what you were thinking yourself, Max—we could defuse Bernardo's ardor by telling him that Allegra and I are betrothed."

"Betrothed! What can you be thinking?" Allegra exploded, causing two female passersby to peer at her intently and then move on, their heads pressed together as they giggled and whispered to each other.

Valerian looked down at her, seeing her flushed cheeks and overbright eyes. "Is it so inconceivable?" he asked as Max continued to busy himself with the basket of violets. "Am I so old and undesirable that Bernardo wouldn't believe you could ever marry me?"

"Don't be so silly, for you are not old at all, even with your angel wings." Allegra sighed, reluctant to explain the obvious, for she had just told Max that Valerian was brilliant. "But only think, Valerian, if an ocean couldn't stop Bernardo, how do you suppose a betrothal could do what the ocean could not? No, he will only bring out his silver mallet and tap-tap on your head as he did on Erberto's, and then the chase will be on once more. No, I think, Valerian, that you shall just have to kill Bernardo for me. There simply is no other way."

Max threw back his head and laughed aloud, nearly dislodging his wig. "Kill him! Oh, boyo, she's a colleen after me own heart! You talk of marriage and she talks of murder. Either way, as I see it, my friend, *you're* a dead man."

"Max—" Valerian began warningly.

"Well, I must be going," the wily Irishman broke in quickly, for a lifetime of living by his wits had given him a fine sense of timing when it came to calling it a day. "I'll be around, checking the dock and the stagecoaches just so I can let you know when our love-bedazzled, shoemaker reaches Brighton—if he doesn't get lost and end by landing in Cornwall."

"Where are you staying?" Valerian called after him, reluctant to see Max leave, though why he should feel that way he was at a loss to explain, even to himself. "I might want to reach you."

But Max just kept on moving, disappearing into a nearby alleyway so quickly that Valerian realized it would be impossible to give chase to the man without deserting Allegra in the middle of the flagway.

"Damn the man!" he swore under his breath, then turned to his companion, thoroughly out of charity with her. "Kill him, Allegra? How do you propose for me to go about it, hmm? A knife? A pistol? Or perhaps a heavy brick applied to the back of his head in a darkened alleyway might do the trick. And will you come watch me hang, or would that prove too upsetting, even for your bloodthirsty Italian sensibilities?"

Allegra saw the pain in Valerian's eyes and longed to throw her arms around him, begging his forgiveness. She wanted nothing more from life than to hear his proposal, but not this way, and not for the reason he had given. But he was not to know that. She would die a thousand terrible deaths before she would let him know that!

"Oh, Valerian," she said, turning to retrace their steps to her grandfather's house, her hand tucked tightly around his arm. "Why are you Englishmen so carelessly brave? Bernardo would not think twice before tapping on your head."

Valerian sought to find solace where he could. "So you have turned down my suggestion of a betrothal purely to protect me? It had nothing to do with whether or not you could *ever* consider a betrothal between the two of us?''

She looked up at him, wishing with all her might that she could believe he truly cared how she answered his last question. ''If—if you were to really mean it, Valerian, I suppose I should not be offended by your proposal,'' she answered at last, trying to be very English about the thing while her Italian blood urged her to tell him exactly what was on her mind. ''Would—would you consider asking me for my hand if it weren't for Bernardo?''

Valerian didn't know how to answer. To tell the truth would end his misery once and for all, for he was not so blind as to be unaware that Allegra looked upon him favorably. And there were their shared kisses at the Pavilion to give him hope as well. But he had already decided that she should experience more of life in England before tying herself to a promise she might live to regret.

''Ah, imp,'' he said, seeing Lord Halsey—and temporary rescue—approaching from the opposite direction. ''There are some questions well-behaved young misses just do not ask. Now smile, Allegra, for unless I miss my guess, his lordship is about to compliment you on your performance last night, and as you and Duggy are promised to him for this evening, I suggest you be polite.''

ALLEGRA SAT ALONE in the Dugdale drawing room, nursing her dark mood. Who did Valerian Fitzhugh think he was, to lecture her on proper deportment as if she were some simple-witted dolt? Who did he think he was talking to, a silly schoolroom chit who had never sung for the Bishop of Bologna? And how dared he tease her about quite the most serious question she had ever asked in her life?

She had all but bared her soul to him, right there on the street, and he had laughed at her, then quickly changed the subject, just as if her question had been of no importance. She had been nonplussed by his action, completely at a loss as to how to go on, and could not remember a word Lord Halsey had said to her. Only now, once Valerian had deposited her back at Number 23 Royal Crescent Terrace and run off like the hounds of Hell were after him, could she think of what she should have done.

She should have turned to him, right there on the street, and asked in a very loud, very carrying voice, "But, Valerian, why then did you take me to a private parlor in the Pavilion—with the Regent in residence and my grandfather in the building as well—and kiss me on the mouth, not once, but twice? I do not know all your English rules of propriety, but in Italy you could not do such a thing without either proposing marriage or being prepared to face my grandfather's vengeance. Isn't that right, Lord Halsey?"

Allegra took a large bite of the pastry Betty had filched from the kitchens for her and nodded emphatically. Yes, that's precisely what she should have said. After all, Valerian had compromised her last night. Even *Uncail* Max had said as much. But all Valerian had done today was to parade her about the town like some prize pullet and then weakly offer his proposal only as a way to thwart Bernardo.

Hadn't the man even considered punching the persistent shoemaker on his perfectly sculpted nose and sending the man back to Napoli on the next ship to leave port? Hadn't he given so much as a moment's thought to protecting her in some other way than by offering her a pretend engagement? And if he had really meant his words, why hadn't he repeated them, telling her the truth?

Her head ached with all this civilization. It was so much easier in Italy. People told you what was on their minds—screamed it at you, actually—so that there could be no doubt as to how they felt. Here, in Brighton, everyone merely danced about, saying things that only implied what they meant, only hinted at the thoughts behind the words. Well, she decided, taking another savage bite of the tart, she could be devious too—even more devious than any Englishman—for she had Italian blood in her veins!

"Ah, there you are, cousin," Gideon said, breaking into her thoughts as he entered the drawing room, closing the doors on the empty hallway behind him. "I was just in the morning room with my dearest mama, lamenting to her how I have not seen you above a few precious moments since your great triumph last night at the Pavilion. We are all very proud of our little Italian cousin, you know."

Allegra glared at him. Gideon was a prime example of what she had been thinking. He never said what he meant, and his mocking tone proved it. He didn't care two sticks about her "great triumph" at the Pavilion. And he wasn't proud of her—none of the Kittredges were proud of her. They merely wanted her inheritance. That's why Gideon had sought her out, and that's why he had closed the doors to the hallway as he entered, so that they would not be interrupted. As a matter of fact, if Betty had been correct, the man was probably about to propose to her.

She felt her temper rising. Two insincere proposals in one short day were just too much. Valerian Fitzhugh might not be here for her to vent her spleen on but Gideon was. She sat back, prepared to make him pay for what he was about to do. It was time she showed these English amateurs what the word *devious* really meant!

"Good afternoon, Gideon," Allegra began, smiling brightly even as her stomach did a small sick flip, for it was not really in her nature to be cruel. She laid the half-eaten strawberry tart back on the plate, her appetite gone, and went on the attack. "Are you here to propose to me, *cugino?*"

"What?" Gideon threw back his handsome head and laughed aloud. "Whatever gave you that idea, cousin?" he asked, slipping his body close beside hers on the settee. "Oh, dear. Has my dearest sister been tattling? I suppose I have been caught out. She heard me baring my soul to Mama yesterday, I suppose, telling her of my deep affection for you, and my hopes for the future. How terrible of Isobel to betray me, not that I should be surprised. She lives to make me suffer for her own well-deserved unhappiness."

He had recovered from his shock so swiftly, lied so smoothly, that Allegra was forced to admire him. "And are you suffering very badly with this great love you bear me, Gideon?'' she asked, picking at the tart once more, for her appetite had reappeared as quickly as it had gone into hiding. ''Please, you must tell me everything.''

Gideon needed no encouragement, his arm snaking out to rest lightly against her spine. This was going to be even easier than he could have hoped. It was his handsome face, he was sure. His handsome face, and his brilliant tailor.

''I was struck by your great beauty the day Fitz-hugh and Uncle Denny dropped you into our laps, my fiery darling, but I knew I had to wait before I could dare to speak of my love.''

''And I was much struck by you, Gideon,'' Allegra answered truthfully, gazing down at her hands, which she had demurely folded in her lap. She had been struck—by his arrogance and total lack of human feeling, not that she was about to tell him that.

Gideon took courage from Allegra's admission and pressed on. ''Mama, bless her generous heart, has already given us her blessing, saying that nothing could be more fitting than to have her only niece's child and her own child united in marriage. Tell me, Allegra—dare I hope?''

Allegra knew she was being naughty, but she was also thoroughly out of charity with all men at the moment, and banished any lingering doubt as to what she would do. ''Hope, Gideon? You are daring to hope?'' She studiously removed his hand from her waist. ''I think, *cugino,* you are daring *many* things. Have you approached my *nonno* and asked his blessing?''

"Uncle Denny?" Gideon leaned back, crossing one well-tailored leg over the other. "Actually, my sweet, I had hoped you might do that for me. You know how Uncle Denny feels about me. He might just cut up stiff if I were to ask him. But he likes you, don't he? He'd accept our engagement, coming from you."

Now she had him. Gideon had swallowed the bait and all that was left was to reel him in. Allegra hid a smile by taking another bite of her snack. "But, *dearest,*" she said, blinking rapidly, "I could not do that. *Nonno* must hear the question from your mouth." She pressed her fingertips against his lips as he tried to protest. "No, no, do not say anything else. Not another word. I cannot promise my hand, I cannot even promise to listen to your proposal—which you have not yet presented—until you have gained permission from *Nonno* to court me."

Gideon leapt to his feet, his eyes haunted. "But he'll skin me alive! He'll throw me out of the house! Think, Allegra! Could you bear for that to happen to the man you love?"

Her furious blinks had done their job, and she produced a single sparkling tear. "Ah, Gideon, you break my heart!" she exclaimed in her best tragic voice. "If you cannot fight for me—" Her voice broke and she buried her face in her handkerchief.

Gideon stood very still, considering his options. He wouldn't fight for Allegra—or anyone, for that matter—if it were his only means to Heaven. However, for a plum, and for the rest of the Dugdale fortune (which would be his the moment he deposited his mother and sister in some far-off cottage in the north of England), he would consider walking through fire in his stockinged feet. Of course—being Gideon— more than anything else, he would consider lying to get what he wanted!

Dropping to one knee in front of her, he vowed fervently, "I will do as you say. I'll promise him that I will never set foot in a gaming house again. I'll give up my friends, the ones he says are leading me to rack and ruin. I'll never lay another wager on a horse race, no matter what the odds. Anything! I'll promise him anything. Only please, Allegra, promise *me* that your answer will be yes!"

"Really, Gideon? You would do this? You would do this for me?"

Gideon swallowed hard. "I will do this!"

Her grandfather was going to enjoy the coming conversation, Allegra consoled herself, picturing Gideon on his knees in front of his uncle, promising to mend his wicked ways.

She turned her head to one side, the handkerchief now clutched dramatically against her breast as she struck a theatrical pose. "No! I cannot! This is wonderful, but I cannot say another word of what lies in my heart, *dear* Gideon, until you have *returned* from *Nonno* with his blessing. Please—I beg you—do not ask me again!"

She held out her hand for his kiss, and continued to hold it out until he belatedly grasped it and pressed his lips to her palm, an action that set her teeth on edge. "I will do as you ask, Allegra, but you must give me time. A few days? A week?"

"I shall not smile again, nor even breathe, until it is done," she vowed earnestly, stealing a line from a very bad play she had once seen in Rome. "Now go," she added, remembering another line from the play, "before my tortured emotions betray me."

Gideon rose, unable to resist the need to brush off the knee of his new fawn breeches. "Thank you, Allegra. Thank you for making me the happiest of men," he declared, turning on his heel and heading, shoulders back, head erect, for the door.

Once she was alone again, Allegra gave way to a fit of the giggles. "I so love Italian opera, even as it is done by silly Englishmen," she said aloud, taking another bite of her strawberry tart just as Isobel—who had seen her brother in the hall and said something nasty to him, only to have him ignore her—entered the room, looking perplexed.

"Was my brother just in here, Allegra?" she asked, taking up a chair on the other side of the small table that sat in front of the settee.

"Yes, indeed, my cousin was here," Allegra answered, still trying to control her happiness, for she was feeling quite pleased with herself, and rather vindicated. "And now you are here. It is so nice to have so many visitors. Will my *zia* Agnes be joining us, do you think? No? Ah, well. Would you like one of these strawberry tarts, *cugina?* Betty got them for me from the kitchens when the cook turned her back. They are very good."

Isobel primly denied the offer. "Perhaps if you did not love food so much, cousin, you would not have so many unseemly bulges in your gowns," she suggested, eyeing Allegra's ample breasts while ignoring the evidence of the other girl's slim waist. "But I am not here to remind you of your faults, dear girl. I am here to congratulate you on your triumph at the Pavilion. Uncle Denny has told us all about it, and I have seen myself the multitude of invitations that have already been stacked high on the mantel. You must be feeling rather smug."

Allegra, who was in fact feeling very smug indeed, only smiled, waving her hands as if dismissing the fuss that her singing had caused. "You are too kind, Isobel. But it is true enough, I suppose. Everyone wants me to sing for them now." Isobel's insults she would ignore, for she could not bring herself to care what the other girl thought.

Isobel, her eyes narrowing, leaned forward, saying, "Yes, they do, don't they? I think it is so unfair of them, to ask you to sing for your supper—to give your talents away for nothing—when you were so celebrated in Italy. That is why," she continued, sneaking a quick look toward the hallway, "I have come to you—to suggest a way you can make them all pay for such shabby treatment."

Allegra frowned, taken off her guard. Isobel acted as if the fashionable people of Brighton had insulted her and she—her loving English cousin—resented it. "But, Isobel, *Nonno* didn't seem to think anything was wrong. Nor did Valerian. Besides, I have no need of money anymore."

Isobel shook her head. "I know that. They are only men, and see no more than the obvious. But just think, Allegra. There are still so many poor soldiers, back from the war all these years, and still without the payment promised them by that fat old man in the Pavilion. Wouldn't it be wonderful if you could do something to ease their pain? Valerian would be greatly pleased, for I have heard him speak so eloquently about the horrors suffered by those wretched men. Valerian has many of them in his employ, you know—men without eyes, men who have lost limbs.''

Allegra, remembering Tweed, Valerian's one-eyed coachman, was hard-pressed not to be carried along on the flood tide of her emotions. She would give anything to help other people. She would give anything to please Valerian. But she was not so simpleminded that she did not recognize that Isobel was purposely directing her along a path she, Isobel, had chosen.

"Please, *cugina,* go on," she begged, for she did long to hear exactly what was on the other girl's mind. It appeared that Gideon was not the only devious Kittredge in the household.

Isobel smiled in unholy glee, which was truly a painful thing to watch. "Then you are interested in my idea! How wonderful! What I have in mind is for you to give a performance—just a single performance—at the Theatre Royal in the New Road.''

It was becoming clear now, Isobel's plan. "But *cugina,* if I were to charge money I would be singing professionally again. Valerian has most expressly requested that I do not do that.''

Isobel hastened to reassure her. "No, no, Allegra. Listen to me! It would not be that way. You would not be keeping the money. It would go for the poor soldiers, the widows, the orphans. You would be a saint!''

She would be ruined for life! She would be thrown out of Society, her grandfather would cut her off without a penny, and a life spent with Bernardo behind his little shoemaker shop would begin to seem a blessing. Allegra leaned forward, smiling. ''A saint, Isobel? I would so like to be a saint.''

''Then you'll do it?''

Isobel, Allegra thought, would starve if she ever chose to go on the stage, for the girl had no talent for playing a part. Her greed and her envy and her longing to destroy her cousin were all quiet clearly stamped on her thin face.

Allegra rose, turning toward the door. ''I will think about it most carefully, Isobel,'' she promised, then turned back to her cousin as inspiration, suddenly her friend, struck yet again. If it had worked once, she reasoned quickly, would it not work twice? ''Yes, dear cousin, I *will* think about it—but only if you go to my *nonno* and ask him for me if the performance would be all right with him.''

''*Me?*'' Isobel's smile disappeared in a heartbeat. ''You want me to ask him? But, Allegra, Uncle Denny barely even *speaks* to me!''

Allegra set her chin defiantly. ''As I told your dear brother just a few minutes ago, I do nothing without my *nonno*'s blessing, no matter how much I may wish it.'' She unbent a little and leaned down to look Isobel squarely in the eye. ''You will do this for me, *cugina?* Besides,'' she added just for good measure, ''I do *so* wish to please Valerian.''

Hearing Allegra speak Fitzhugh's name lent new starch to Isobel's spine. That, and the mention of her hated brother's name in almost the same breath.

"Gideon is going to approach Uncle Denny—for your hand?" she guessed, knowing that if the Baron agreed to the match, she would no longer need to destroy Allegra's chances with Valerian by making her a laughingstock in front of all of Brighton. Not that she had much faith in her mama's estimation of Gideon's ability to talk Allegra around to marrying him—which was why she had felt it imperative that she come up with a plan of her own. "And then you will accept him? If he gets Uncle Denny's permission?"

Allegra's sapphire eyes all but danced in her head as she leaned even closer and asked, "You can keep a secret, dearest Isobel?"

"Yes, yes! Anything!" Isobel answered, her heart pounding with excitement.

"You will swear it on your eyes?" Allegra persisted. "Think, *cugina,* for this is a very dangerous curse to wish on yourself. Italian curses often are, you know."

Isobel shivered, crossing her fingers behind her back. "I swear. On my eyes," she whispered hoarsely.

"Then I will tell you," Allegra answered brightly. "Yes, Gideon is going to ask *Nonno* for his permission to woo me. And no, I shall not marry him. I could not do this, you see, because I have already decided to marry Valerian."

Isobel's eyes all but popped out of her head at exactly the same time that her stomach plummeted to her toes. "Valerian! Do not tell me Valerian has asked you to be his wife?"

Allegra dismissed this question with a wave of her hand. "No. But he will. He loves me, *sotto sotto*— deep down. He just does not know it yet, I think, poor man."

This was all very confusing to Isobel, whose full concentration had been on her own plan, so that she could not see that Allegra was playing out a small stratagem of her own. "Then I truly don't understand. Why did you allow Gideon to hope in the first place? It seems very cruel."

"I did it because Gideon does not love me, but only the plum I will receive when I marry. I did it, dearest Isobel, because I wish to watch as your silly brother puffs himself up to a great height, only to collapse into a great airless heap. I think *Nonno* will not be so nice to him either, and that also pleases me. Does it please you?"

"Oh, yes," Isobel responded earnestly, rubbing her hands together. If Allegra didn't stand in the way of her happiness with Valerian, Isobel might even think she was beginning to like her Italian cousin. "And it serves him right too, trying to use you to pay off his horrible gambling debts."

Then she sobered, realizing that Allegra's admission took them both back to the question of Valerian. She would have no choice but to continue with her plan to disgrace Allegra if Gideon's suit was destined to be denied. But even Isobel was not so thick as to overlook the obvious. "And why are you sending *me* to Uncle Denny, Allegra? Are you hoping he will not be nice to me either?''

Allegra did her best to appear puzzled by the question. ''And why would that be, Isobel? You said yourself that I would be doing a great thing, singing for all those widows and the tiny *bambinos*. Surely *Nonno* will not object to your most wonderful idea. But you see, because *Nonno* loves me and wishes to make up for leaving me abandoned all these years, he may give his agreement just to please me, which is something I could not let him do. So you must ask him for me, just as if *I* knew nothing about the plan.

''Besides,'' she added, in case her reason hadn't completely convinced Isobel, ''your English, um, *she* is so much better than mine. *Comprende?* And *Nonno* does admire you so much for your great intelligence—as well as your beauty. I have seen it in his eyes when you talk to him.''

''Yes,'' Isobel answered hesitantly, preening a bit at the inferred compliment, ''I suppose you're right about all that, but—''

''Then it is settled!'' Allegra bent to kiss Isobel on both cheeks. ''I shall be so eager to hear that you have done me this small favor so that I might give my concert. We must devise a special invitation for the Regent, don't you think?''

''Missy?''

Leaving Isobel to muddle through everything that had gone on, Allegra turned to see Betty standing by the open doors, looking decidedly nervous. ''You said for me to tell you when your new bonnet got here.''

Her new bonnet? Allegra didn't have the faintest

notion of what Betty was telling her. She looked at the maid and asked carefully, "And which bonnet would that be, Betty?"

Betty spoke through clenched teeth, surreptitiously motioning with her right hand—the one that held a folded sheet of paper. "The *Irish* green bonnet, missy, if you take my meaning. It's at the servants' door right now, waiting on you."

Allegra shot a quick look at Isobel, who seemed lost in a brown study. She would have loved to stay a while and watch her cousin attempt to puzzle out what had happened in the past ten minutes, but she had more important things to do now than to amuse herself by turning the tables on Isobel and Gideon Kittredge's plans for her future.

"If you'll excuse me, Isobel?" she asked, already heading for the hallway.

"Yes, yes, you go on now," Isobel answered vaguely, her mind concentrating on precisely how she was going to present her plan for the Baron's permission and at the same time make him think the whole thing had been her mother's idea.

CHAPTER NINE

BETTY WAS still occupied in helping Allegra don her cherry-red cloak as the younger woman entered the kitchens.

"I cannot believe it. He is arrived so soon?" Allegra questioned, seeing Max seated at his ease at the table, a fresh strawberry tart in his hand, the bottom half of his face hidden behind a truly glorious red beard.

"Love sails on wings, I suppose, m'darlin'," Max answered, holding out his arm as he rose and began walking toward the servants' entrance.

"Missy!" Betty cried, wringing her hands as she watched her mistress leaving on the Irishman's arm. "Whatever am I to say to the Baron iffen he should ask for you?"

"Lock my door and tell everyone who asks that I am lying down with the headache," Allegra offered quickly, turning to face down a lingering scullery maid and the Dugdale cook. "And if *anyone* is heard to say differently, Betty, give me their names and I will call down a most terrible curse upon their heads, so that their betraying tongues fall out and all their fingers tie themselves into knots. I am *Italiana*, and I can do these things!"

The Dugdale servants, one of them visibly quaking while the other quickly made the sign against the evil eye, both promised not to breathe a word of what they had seen, and as Max chuckled his delight at her ingenuity, Allegra quit the house for the alleyway.

"Where is Bernardo now? Have you sent a messenger to Valerian? He has gone back to his estate, yes? I am sure he has, as we did not expect the shoemaker so soon as this. Have you put Bernardo where no one can see him? Do you think anyone will recognize me with my hood pulled down this way? Yesterday I should not have worried, but today I am famous, you know. Oh, everything is happening so quickly!"

Max was huffing and puffing, having some difficulty keeping up with both the pace Allegra was setting and her rapid-fire questions. "Bernardo is safely tucked up in my room at a small inn near Chapel Street, though it wasn't an easy thing, don't you know, to talk him out of running up and down every street in Brighton, calling your name. It's a determined fellow he is, your shoemaker."

"He is not *my* shoemaker, *Uncail* Max," Allegra corrected, ducking her head as a familiar face passed by. "But you have not told me about Valerian. Will he be meeting us at this inn?"

Max would have laughed, but he was rapidly getting out of breath. "And thereby hangs a tale! Valerian was the one what brought Bernardo to me. It's underestimating the boy I've been doin', I think. Not only did he ferret out the place where I'm staying, but he beat me to Bernardo as well. And, bless him, the fellow already has cooked up a plan to explain the shoemaker's presence until we might straighten this thing out once and for all. It's a very good plan it is, too, if only we can pull it off, which I've no doubt we can. Do you think, mayhap, there might be a drop of the Irish in Valerian? Yes, a fine broth of a boy!''

They were nearing the waterfront and Max prudently took a quick peep behind them before pulling Allegra into a narrow alleyway and entering the third door on the left.

Together they tiptoed down the hall past the inn's common room and climbed the staircase to the top of the high narrow house, to come to Max's room. The Irishman knocked twice, waited, then knocked twice more before Valerian opened the door to allow Max and Allegra to step inside.

Instantly all was chaos.

Bernardo, who had been slumped dejectedly beside a sloping wooden table, his elbows on his knees, spotted the love of his life and leapt to his feet, his smile so wide and blightingly white that Valerian felt obliged to turn away.

Allegra, in her turn, espied the shoemaker and instantly burst into a scathing stream of Italian that had a lot to do with the great disrespect with which she regarded Bernardo's brainpower and little to do with greeting a fellow countryman who had come to the English shore.

As Bernardo stood there, a glorious, sad-eyed angel whose wrists stuck out a full two inches from the bottom of his coat sleeves, Allegra continued her assault, her musical voice rising and falling as she berated the shoemaker with a barrage of insults, her entire body taking part in the tongue-lashing as she gave emphasis to her words with expressive hand gestures and eloquent shrugs.

She finally ran down, ending her scolding with a stern warning to Bernardo that if he so much as tried to utter a single word in his own defense she would personally see to it that her good friend, the Prince Regent, had him hauled to the very top of the Marine Pavilion and then deposited, rump down, on the extreme tip of the largest, most pointed onion dome on the entire building.

Max collapsed onto the side of the narrow bed, wiping his brow. "Ah, and it's grand to listen to her when she's in a rage, isn't it? Takes the cockles off m'heart, don't you know."

Exhausted by her own vehemence, Allegra subsided into the chair Bernardo had vacated and began fanning herself with a handkerchief she had pulled from the pocket of her gown.

"Brava! Brava!" Valerian applauded from the vantage point he had taken up in front of the single window in the small, meanly furnished room. "I begin to think, imp, that you give your most impassioned performances in ramshackle inns, although I see your months in civilization have robbed you of the ability to spit in order to lend credence to your threats. I hesitated to point that out, but I find that, since meeting you, I must take my pleasures where I might find them."

"Valerian!" Allegra ran to him, throwing herself

against his broad chest, and tightly wrapped her arms about his waist. She had temporarily forgotten Fitzhugh in her sudden, overwhelming anger upon seeing Bernardo standing in the room big as life, grinning as if she would actually be pleased to see him.

From his position in the middle of the room, Bernardo began to growl low in his throat, one hand going beneath his shirt in search of his metal mallet—the same metal mallet Valerian had prudently demanded the man put into his keeping earlier, before he would agree to allow Max to fetch Allegra.

"*Arrah* now, do sit down, you beautiful dolt," Max ordered from the bed. "You're becoming a bloody nuisance one way or the other, don't you know? And what are you glowering at in the first place? Can't you see you've lost her? All that remains now is to ship you straight home again before anybody here becomes the wiser, for it's a fine mess you could make for this sweet colleen, and no mistake, even if Fitzhugh here has a plan, which I'm thinkin' now might not be so good as it first seemed."

As if the words had conjured up the deed, the door to the room burst open and Gideon Kittredge stepped inside to look about, his avid gaze taking in all of the occupants. "My, my, and what do we have here, hmm? I thought I saw you pass by the coffeehouse, and I was right. That's ten pounds Georgie Watson owes me." He put a hand to his ear. "Listen? Do you hear that, cousin? Ah, what a pity. It's the sound of my dear uncle's bellow, calling for his solicitor so that he can change his will yet again."

It was Max who spoke first, shaking his head sadly.

"Candie is right, boyo, and it's getting past it I must be. I had no idea we were being followed. It's that sorry I am, don't you know."

"Valerian?" Allegra questioned quietly, her eyes wide with apprehension as she looked up at him. Everything was becoming so confused.

"Just be very quiet, imp, and we may wriggle out of this yet. It's time to put my plan, such as it is, into action," he answered softly as he gently disengaged her death grip around his waist and stepped forward, his hand outstretched, to welcome Gideon to their little gathering.

Gideon's hand came out automatically, although his eyes remained puzzled as he stared at Bernardo, who, unbelievably, appeared to be even prettier than he, as if that were possible. "Fitzhugh," he said blankly. "What are you doing here? Who are these people? Isn't m'cousin here for an assignation with that bearded fellow over there? I don't understand."

"You *don't* understand, do you?" Max sniffed indelicately, although it had to have pleased him that Gideon believed that he, who would never again see the sunny side of fifty, might be having an "assignation" with a young, beautiful colleen like Allegra. "And there's nothing so surprising in that, I'll be thinking, you miserable buckeen, for you have the look of one what has a great deal of knowledge outside his head."

"Quiet, Max," Valerian warned softly, motioning Gideon to a chair. A lot depended on these next minutes and he disliked having his concentration broken by the Irishman's wit. "Now, Gideon, I suppose you'd like to know what's going on here. Of course you would, as would I if our positions were reversed.''

''Yes, well, I suppose so!'' Gideon sat briefly, made to rise, then sat down once more, all the time staring at Bernardo. ''Is that fellow *real*, Valerian? He looks like a painting.''

The shoemaker, who had been blessedly silent for so long, took it into his head at this moment to add his mite to the conversation. *''Il mio nome é,''* he announced proudly, rising to his full, impressive height and jabbing one long forefinger into his chest as he introduced himself, ''Bernardo Sansone Guglielmo Alonso Timoteo—''

''Conte Timoteo to you, Gideon,'' Valerian broke in quickly, unceremoniously pushing Bernardo back down into his chair and stepping in front of the shoemaker before the fool totally destroyed Allegra by adding ''premier shoemaker of Milano!''

Gideon peered past Valerian to take in Bernardo's humble garb. ''Conte Timoteo? Shouldn't he dress better than that? Not that my tailor would have him, of course. He has far too many muscles to allow a jacket to lie smoothly. And look at his thighs. They're positively obscene. As a matter of fact, Valerian, I think the only thing good about him is those boots. Magnificent work, don't you think?''

Bernardo, whose command of the English language thankfully remained somewhat limited, stuck out one boot and beamed a smile at Gideon. ''My *stivali? Sì.* He is *magnifico!''*

A sharp explosion of rapid-fire Italian from Allegra

silenced the shoemaker and he lowered his head, giving in once more to the overwhelming sorrow of at last acknowledging that the single great love of his life refused to love him back. He was lost, at sea—adrift without a hint as to what would become of him now. His hope gone, his brother and cousin calling him mad and deserting him to return to the shoemaker shop, Bernardo had nowhere to go, nothing to live for, and nothing—considering the sad, empty state of his pockets—to live on even if he should wish to go on living, which, of course, he did not.

He would have to fling himself into the cold, dark sea. He would have to end it all, a broken-hearted shell of a man who could not find anything left in all the world to give him hope. He would—"*Che cosa?*" Bernardo's head snapped up. What was it the tall man with the silver wings in his hair had said? *Conte Timoteo?* Who was *Conte* Timoteo?

Bernardo straightened in the chair and began to listen very carefully to what Valerian was telling the skinny, flour-white-skinned man who had admired his boots.

"...and so you see, Gideon, Allegra's cousin, the Conte, had no choice but to apply to his only remaining relative for assistance. His house and grounds lost to him in a debt of honor—surely you of all people can understand the Conte's need to satisfy his gaming debts—he spent his last penny, even sold his wardrobe, to procure passage for his loyal servant, Max, and himself to come to Brighton."

Max growled low in his throat, but Valerian silenced him with a look.

"To continue," Valerian said firmly, redirecting his attention to Gideon, a young man in whom the light of knowledge did not, thankfully, burn brightly. "Not wishing to embarrass his cousin by showing up at the Baron's door in his shabby clothes, he sent Max to bring Allegra to him. It is all quite simple, really, when you think about it. Oh, yes, the only thing the Conte could not bear to part with was his magnificent boots," he added as an afterthought. "It seems we men, too, can be vain."

Kittredge scratched at the side of his head, looking toward Allegra, who was at that moment whispering into Bernardo's ear—a far happier Bernardo than the shoemaker had been a few moments earlier.

Clearly Gideon had misunderstood the situation. Everything was still all right. He could still approach his uncle Denny for Allegra's money—no! He gave a slight shake to his head, making a mental erasure. He could approach him for Allegra's *hand*—he must remember to ask for her *hand!* It would appear he had some more work to do on the speech he had been preparing with Georgie Watson at the coffeehouse.

"Yes, yes, I think I understand now," Gideon mumbled at last, just as Max, who had been growing impatient with Kittredge's excruciatingly slow mental processes, had been about to explode in frustration. "But I still don't understand what *you're* doing here, Valerian."

As Valerian hesitated—for he had not taken his plan far enough to consider what he would say if they were caught out here at the inn—Allegra, whose father had often praised her for her ability to cover beautifully for another singer who suffered a mental lapse on stage, stepped forward to effect a rescue.

"Max—*Cugino* Bernardo's valet—summoned Valerian before he came for me. My *cugino* and Valerian had met in Milano, you see, at the Palazzo dell'Ambrosiana, and it was he, my *cugino,* who helped him to locate me in Firenze in the first place. *Capisce?* Do you understand now, Gideon?"

This overabundance of Italian proved to be too much for Gideon, who only nodded, saying, "Yes, I see. I see—I think."

Allegra, flushed with her success, continued. "And that is why I was hugging dear Valerian when you came in, Gideon. Valerian, being such a dear, dear friend, had just offered to house Bernardo and clothe him until such time as his so-very-sickly uncle passes away—an uncle on his mother's side, so that I, unfortunately, cannot share in the bounty—and Bernardo inherits the man's fortune and can return to his own estates. It is all quite simple, yes?"

Valerian, who had, halfway through Allegra's speech, turned to her in mingled astonishment and dismay, belatedly found his voice. Speaking through clenched teeth, he said, "So if you don't mind keeping our secret until the Conte is better outfitted to meet the Baron, perhaps we can get on with it. I would like to quit this room as soon as possible. Can I trust you to escort your cousin home, Gideon?"

By now Bernardo understood as much as he, with his already remarked-upon limited brain-power, would probably ever understand. He had lost his beloved Allegra. But he had gained a title, and new clothes, and something to eat besides the moldy bit of cheese that was all he had left in his pocket, and could even look forward to having a roof to cover his head that night. Wasn't he a lucky shoemaker? Wasn't this England wonderful?

His smile bright, Bernardo exuberantly dashed about hugging everyone and soundly kissing them on both cheeks—including a thoroughly disgusted Gideon, who made short work of extricating both Allegra and himself from the room.

As Valerian stood looking at the door that had just closed behind Allegra's back, Max walked up to him, rested a hand on his shoulder, and said, "That little girl can spout lies that would shame a tinker, Lord love her. Now, boyo, my *master* has need of at least three suits of clothes, excluding his evening dress, and all of the other bits and pieces that go with them. I'll have the shops send the bills round to you, but I shall be needin' a bit of the ready to tide me over, don't you know."

Valerian looked down at the pudgy Irishman and the hand the man was holding out to him and saw the gleam in the man's eyes. "We'll do this shopping together. Much as you might think my brains have been addled by all that has gone on here, Max, I'm not so confused as to give you carte blanche with my money.

"But first," he said, picking up his cloak and motioning for the still grinning Bernardo to follow him, "I think we might stop downstairs and split a few bottles. Perhaps I am just getting old, but I am suddenly very much in need of a drink."

"A cup of the creature wouldn't do any of us harm, I'm thinkin'," Max agreed readily, turning to Bernardo. "*Vino,* you paper-skulled Adonis?"

Bernardo nodded emphatically, tossing his tattered cloak and small worn satchel into Max's arms just as if he had lived his entire life surrounded by servants. He lifted his head imperiously and brushed past Valerian, to be the first through the doorway. "*Vino, sì! Vino* for Bernardo—*Conte Timoteo!*"

Valerian laughed out loud. "Taking his heart-break rather well, isn't he, Max?" he suggested, following the shoemaker.

Bringing up the rear, loaded down with Bernardo's belongings, Maximilien Murphy launched himself into a string of Irish curses that could have blasted a hole in an iron pot.

"ODDS FISH! *Say that again, boy! I don't believe I'm hearing this!*"

Baron Dugdale's incredulous roar could be heard throughout the house, and everyone within earshot raced to discover what had happened, each harboring her own fears—and even hopes—as to precisely what had launched the Baron into the boughs.

Isobel had been sitting alone in the drawing room, still carefully composing the impassioned plea she would employ to convince her uncle that Allegra should perform for money, while still letting him know that the inspiration behind this glorious idea came from something her mother had said—just in case Uncle Denny should cut up stiff at the idea.

Her arguments, already three days in the making,

were starting to sound feasible even to her, so that Isobel was beginning to harbor serious doubts that a charity performance by Allegra would have the expected result—that of forever disgracing her cousin in Valerian's eyes.

But what other choice did she have open to her? Allegra had already told her that she would never accept a proposal from Gideon—who was even now closeted with her uncle—because she expected to receive an offer from Valerian. And Isobel would die, simply die, if that were ever to happen.

But if Isobel were to approach her uncle with the idea of a charity performance, and if that stupid Prince Regent should give it his blessing, the whole thing could end with Valerian being even more in charity with Allegra than he was at this moment. In which case—and this was the point that bothered Isobel most of all—why should her mother get the credit for thinking of such a wonderful idea in the first place while she, Isobel, the true genius, received no recognition at all?

The Baron's bellow had interrupted these tortured thoughts and Isobel had run into the hallway, only to cannon into her mother, who had just dashed from the morning room, twin dots of color giving life to her otherwise sallow face.

"Look out, you little idiot!" Agnes screeched, hastily pushing her daughter to one side, so that Isobel was forced to pick up her skirts and run behind her mother, each of them fighting to be in the lead.

Agnes, who had been mentally redecorating the morning room with some of the plum that would come to her the day Gideon and Allegra were wed, and who knew that her beloved son was with her brother at that moment, immediately thought the *worst*—which, she supposed, grinning, might just as easily turn out to be the *best!*

Obviously, Agnes told herself as she and Isobel (now side by side, as youth and speed had little difficulty overcoming age and greed) ran toward the study door, Denny had exploded in wrath at the mere idea of Gideon marrying his granddaughter. That was most probably to be expected, she knew, although still depressingly ignorant of the man. Why couldn't her brother bring himself to see the obvious—that her son was the most wonderful, lovable creature on earth, and his precious Allegra should thank her lucky stars that he should deign to toss his cap her way.

But if the worst were to happen and the Baron denied the suit, the strain of screaming at her son caused by her brother's inevitable anger might prove to be too much for the man's heart. Why, even now her dearest Denny could be prostrate on the floor, breathing his last. A plum was lovely, but to gain the entire inheritance in one blow was even lovelier!

Unless, of course, as Gideon had supposed, the dratted man had summoned his solicitor again and already changed his will! That chilling thought lent wings to Agnes's steps, and it was only with some difficulty that Allegra, who had been descending the staircase at the moment her grandfather had called out—Betty having told her that Gideon was meeting with the man, and eager to listen at the door while her *nonno* tore a verbal strip off the younger man's hide—was able to be the one to throw open the door to the study.

The trio of women took two steps inside and skidded to a halt to survey the damage.

The Baron was not either clutching his chest in pain or collapsed in his chair, which greatly depressed Agnes's hopes for recovering the morning room chairs in the lovely gold brocade material she had seen in that little shop on Dean Street.

Gideon, it would seem, however, hadn't fared nearly so well as his still upright uncle, for he was on his knees in front of the fireplace, his forearms pressed protectively against the top of his head.

Isobel, who had come to a halt just behind Allegra, twisted up her mouth in disgust, not as disappointed by her brother's failure to gain permission to woo Allegra as she was by her own momentary hope that the simpleton might have somehow pulled it off and Allegra, who seemed to place so much faith in her grandfather's judgment, would then agree to go along with the engagement.

Lastly, there was Allegra, the architect of the scene that was even now playing itself out in the Dugdale study. She, if anyone were to apply to her at the moment for her thoughts, would have announced herself greatly pleased with the sight of Gideon groveling on the hearth.

Even if she hadn't already wished her arrogant cousin at the opposite end of the earth, his actions of the past three days—days that had dragged along interminably, as neither Valerian nor Bernardo had yet to present themselves at Number 23—had proved to her that no punishment that befell Gideon could be too terrible.

For Gideon had been making her life a misery ever since discovering her at the inn with Bernardo, plaguing her with questions about "her cousin the Conte" for which she had no answers. How rich would the Conte be when his sick uncle died? And if the Conte were to die—perish at sea or some such thing on his way back to Italy—would his money then go to her, Gideon's wife? And then there was this palace of the Conte's to consider. Were there many servants? How many bedrooms did it have? It was the outside of enough! Gideon, she was sure, was so greedy he must have heard the coins jingling in his mother's pockets before he was born!

The Baron belatedly became aware of his feminine audience, bowed, and pointed to his kneeling nephew with the tip of his cane. "Come to see the show, have you, eh? It seems everybody but me was privy to what this ignorant puppy was about, yipping around my heels with his blasted proposals. Here, now, boy," he said, prodding at Gideon's shoulder with the cane, "let's hear that last part again, so that everyone can see how low you can sink."

Gideon turned his head to see his mother, sister, and cousin standing just behind him. He looked up at his uncle, his eyes silently pleading with the man not to put him through this torture. He had tried and failed. He had lost a fortune, and most probably his mother's good graces. Wasn't that enough? Did he have to be made a figure of fun in front of his sister, who looked to be enjoying every second of his disgrace?

Taking refuge in the tried-and-true, Gideon put a hand to his mouth and coughed.

"Oh, never mind!" the Baron growled in disgust, lifting the cane so that Gideon could rise. "Tell a lie once and it lives forever, I say. There's no need to hear all that drivel again. You, Aggie—you're the one who's behind this anyway, unless I miss my guess. *He* don't have the wit to think up such nonsense by himself. Did you really think I'd believe this worthless scamp could ever stop his gaming and be a good husband to my granddaughter here? I'd as soon believe Prinny will send word to Calais tomorrow to fetch Brummell back for another go at being his bosom beau! Now get out of here—the lot of you. Except you, Allegra. I want to talk to you."

"Perhaps you'd best consider a repairing lease at Papa's cousin Bertrand's in Wolverhampton, Gideon, until your creditors forget you," Isobel suggested happily as her brother brushed past her, coughing into his hand. Agnes quickly followed him out of the room, mumbling something about having Betty fetch the lad's restorative tonic.

"You're a cruel, unnatural child, Isobel," her mother took the time to declare feeling, which only served to make Isobel laugh out loud as she closed the door.

Once everyone was gone Allegra turned to her grandfather, smiling. "Does your toe pain you, *Nonno?*" she asked, waiting until he sat down before settling herself on the footstool at his feet.

"My toe?" the Baron questioned blankly, looking down at his bandaged foot. "Why, bless me, I do believe it's healed. And to think I didn't even notice, being so busy yelling at that idiot. Imagine him thinking I'd give you over into his keeping! Daft fool! That boy isn't fit to mind mice at a crossroad. Haven't enjoyed anything half so much as seeing him on his knees, though, telling me how he loved you and how he would never go gaming again." He peered intently at his granddaughter. "How did you know the gout was gone?"

Allegra shrugged, smiling in real pleasure. "The cherries helped, I suppose, but I also remembered something my father once told me, *Nonno.* He said that a happy man, a laughing man, has no room inside him for pain. You see, the proposal was not all *Zia* Agnes's idea, for I allowed Gideon to hope I would agree to a match between us if he came first to you."

"Eh? And why would you do a thing like that, child? You couldn't want him."

"Never! I only thought having Gideon ask for my hand might amuse you—although I must not lie. I am also a little naughty, *Nonno,* and wished for you to bellow at Gideon, for I do not much care for him, even if he is your nephew. I did tell you that I am not always nice. You are pleased?"

The Baron, who was not so old that he could not recognize the fine hand of a woman's revenge, threw back his head and laughed aloud. "Odds fish, but that's good! I always thought you *I*-talians were downy ones. Tell me, child, do you have any plans for that scheming Aggie—or that die-away daughter of hers? You never know when the gout might be back, eh?''

Allegra, who had begun to feel some small remorse for her meanness now that the deed was done, was saved from answering as the butler entered the room, cleared his throat audibly, and announced: "The Conte Timoteo and Mister Fitzhugh to see you, my lord."

THE FOLLOWING TWO HOURS remained mostly a blur in Allegra's memory.

Valerian had handled the introductions brilliantly, beginning with his greeting, which had included the words "Look, dear Allegra, at the *surprise* I have brought you." Taking her cue from him, she had pretended to be astonished by Bernardo's arrival in Brighton, although her astonishment at Bernardo's appearance as he stood in her grandfather's study was not feigned, for Valerian had surely wrought a miracle.

The shoemaker, always handsome, had been transformed into a heavenly vision whose brilliance almost hurt her eyes. His unruly blond locks had been tamed and styled so that they surrounded his face like a gilt picture frame, with a few of the golden ringlets dropping carelessly onto his smooth forehead.

Bernardo's fine body—long, powerful legs and muscular upper torso—had been poured into a modish suit of clothes that, if it were possible for mere fabric to speak, would doubtless thank all the angels and the saints for the opportunity to serve such a glorious purpose.

Perhaps his memory of polite behavior had been prodded by recollecting his years spent as a "companion" to a lonely English lady in Italy, or perhaps it was just that all Italians seem to have a flair for performing—but Bernardo himself had been wonderful.

Saying little, and employing much of his mother tongue, the shoemaker had dazzled the Baron and the Kittredges as well—except, perhaps, for Gideon, who had crept back into the room to stand at a distance and eye Bernardo's expensive tailoring with open envy.

Valerian's explanation for Bernardo's appearance had satisfied the Baron as easily as it had Gideon— for none of the purely English inhabitants of Number 23 was especially acute. Even Agnes fluttered and giggled, and Isobel, who had thought herself hopelessly in love with Valerian, transferred her loyalties to Bernardo within five minutes of his arrival on the scene.

All in all, Bernardo's entry could only be termed a brilliant success. It was only later, while the "Conte Timoteo" and Isobel took a stroll about the garden and Allegra and Valerian stole some time to themselves in the morning room, that Allegra could voice her fears.

"*Nonno* wishes to take Bernardo with us tomorrow to the Pavilion," she told Valerian, her sapphire eyes clouded with apprehension.

"And you are wondering how you will explain the dear Conte's propensity for eating with his fingers?" Valerian offered, seating himself beside her on the striped satin settee. "I admit it might prove difficult. Shall I have him develop the plague, or will a simple inflammation of the lungs be sufficient to have him cry off for the evening?"

Allegra's bottom lip came out in a pout. "Do not make sport of me, Valerian," she commanded testily. "I have not had a very nice day—a very nice several days. Why did you stay away so long?"

"Did you miss me, imp?"

Allegra shot Valerian a look that delighted him no end. Until she spoke. "I need to make a small confession, I suppose. I have been very naughty, Valerian—though it is all your fault."

He raised one eyebrow, looking down at her expectantly. "Of course it is, imp. Heaven forbid you should do anything that is *your* fault."

She sprang up from the settee to begin pacing the carpet and Valerian leaned back, content to admire the sight of his dearest Allegra in a dither. "You were mean to me, Valerian, saying that polite young ladies do not speak of proposals and the like. You remember this, yes? I was very hurt—*very* hurt. And when I am hurt I do not always do nice things, although I am always sorry for them later."

Valerian looked about the room, noticing that all the vases and mirrors were still in one piece. "Is the damage confined to your room, then? I see nothing amiss here."

She rounded on him, her small hands drawn up into fists, her ample breasts heaving in agitation. "*Stupido!* Why must you persist in thinking I know no other way to show anger than to scream or break things? I can be devious, you know. I *was* devious! And I am now so ashamed of myself!'' With that, and totally without warning, she burst into tears, launching herself on Valerian's chest.

It took some time, but at last Valerian succeeded in getting the entire story out of her—all about her plans to pay Gideon out for his lies and greed while punishing Isobel for her scheme to lure Allegra into social disgrace.

He could not, he found, discover in his heart any sympathy for either Kittredge. Gideon had deserved his punishment, and as for Isobel—well, wasn't it true that all was fair in love and war? He did, however— since Allegra had told him *everything*—feel impelled to ask her how she had come to the conclusion that he was going to propose to her.

"You already did!" she exclaimed, now sitting beside him once more and dabbing delicately at her still moist eyes. "Oh, I know it was only to protect me that you thought of it, but you *did* think of it, when there were so many other things you could have done. You did not like me over-much when we were in Italy, as I did not very much like you—but that has changed. You love me now, Valerian.''

Valerian rose, finding that it was now his turn to pace the carpet. It was true. He loved Allegra. He loved her with all his heart, Heaven help him. But he also loved his well-ordered life, the life he had lost the moment he had first learned of her existence. Suddenly, without warning, he felt trapped, backed into a corner.

The devil with his earlier notions that she was too

young to make up her mind about marriage when she had yet to see London, let alone experience a Season. That had only been an excuse he'd used to delay the inevitable. If there was one thing he had learned about Allegra, it was that the child had very definite opinions.

And how could he forget his dreams of traveling the world with her at his side, or his visions of their sons and daughters playing on the lawns of his estate? *He* was the one he had believed to be too young to be tied to a spouse and children.

Yes, she was lovely. Yes, life since meeting her had been exciting. Yes, he dreamed about her at night and looked for her all the day long. Yes, he was fast on his way to becoming obsessed by his longing for this small, exciting, exotic scrap of explosive femininity.

His sigh was so deep and heartfelt that he saw Allegra's hand go out to him, as if he might be ill. There was nothing else for it. He loved her. She had accepted it. Now it was his turn to face it.

Valerian's head came up and his shoulders straightened. His decision had been made, and it was final!

But *he* would do the asking, dammit, when *he* considered the time to be right! That's what was wrong. That was why he felt so trapped. It wasn't that he didn't love her. It was only that she wasn't playing by the rules. If, as the saying went, it was best for one to begin in the way one planned to go on, it was time he took charge of the situation!

"While it is true enough that there were other avenues open to me—killing Bernardo was your suggestion, as I recall—a pretended betrothal merely seemed to be the thing to offer at the time,'' he said at last, deliberately avoiding her eyes. ''But as for loving you, imp—as for wishing to marry you—I'm afraid that *I* must be the one to tell you that—''

He never got to finish his poorly conceived confession, for Allegra was on her feet and running for the doorway, her hands tightly clapped to her ears. She had almost escaped him before he caught up with her, whirling her about to face him.

''Listen to me, imp,'' he begged, seeing tears standing in her eyes once more. ''You think I am rejecting you, when I am only trying to explain how I feel about—''

''No!'' she exclaimed, pushing herself out of his embrace. ''I have made the *idiota* of myself. You were kind to me, and in my foolish vanity I believed that this kindness came from love. Forgive me, Valerian, if I have abused that kindness. *Addio!*''

''Allegra, wait!''

But it was too late. Bernardo, with Isobel hanging from his arm like a limpet attached to a strong outcrop of solid rock, had appeared in the doorway, and all Valerian could do was watch helplessly as Allegra brushed by them and ran upstairs.

CHAPTER TEN

GIDEON HAD, in desperation, retreated to his bed, which was as far from his increasingly demanding creditors as he could conceivably hope to travel without applying to his uncle for funds—a consideration which by itself was enough to make the young man believe that, for once, he was really ill.

Adding to Gideon's melancholy was the all-but-constant presence in the house of Conte Timoteo—and the Conte's wardrobe Gideon found out very rapidly that it is extremely difficult to spend the entirety of one's life believing that one is the most handsome, well-turned-out gentleman in the vicinity, only to have one's own mother and sister fawn over some rosy-cheeked, vacant-eyed Italian who probably didn't understand every third word spoken to him!

If watching his scrawny sister make a cake out of herself hadn't been debilitating enough, his own mother—a woman who had clothed herself in half-mourning for the past sixteen years—had thoroughly sickened him by parading around the house waving an ivory-sticked fan boasting a hand-painted silk rendition of no less than the Coliseum itself!

Yet taking to his bed had not helped. Gideon coughed, and his mama sent Betty with the restorative tonic. Gideon moaned, and his mama told him to be a good little soldier and stuff a handkerchief in his mouth. Gideon asked if he could be set up on the settee in the drawing room, a blanket over his knees, and his mama refused, saying he might then give his latest illness to "our dear Conte, who had just endured an arduous sea voyage."

Why, it was enough to make a grown man healthy.

So it seemed to Gideon that insult was about to be heaped upon injury when there came a knock on his bedchamber door and Allegra peeped her head in to ask if she could speak with him.

"*You!* I know now what you were about. I saw your face when Uncle Denny turned me down. You tricked me. You were never going to marry me. And now you've come to crow over me!" he accused, turning his head toward the windows. "Well, I won't have it, so you can just go away again. Go on—go away!"

Allegra closed the door behind her and walked across the room to the bed. "Poor *bambino*," she sympathized, knowing that he had been at least partially correct. She *had* wanted Gideon to feel the rough side of her grandfather's tongue. She *had* enjoyed it. But that was not why she had come to her cousin's room.

She pulled up a straight-backed chair, taking from it the worn, velvet, floppy-eared rabbit that had been Gideon's since childhood, and sat down, the rabbit in her lap. "Are you feeling very ill, *cugino?*"

Gideon rolled onto his back, his bottom lip jutting out in defiance. "Yes, I am—and a lot anyone around here cares, if I live or die! It's all 'the dear Conte this' and 'the dear Conte that.' I'd like to take that stupid Italian and ship him straight back where he came from!''

"You do not like Bernardo, do you?" Allegra asked, knowing that it was not a brilliant question. "I fear I do not much like him either. He is too puffed up, too full of himself since he came to Brighton. He is a very different Bernardo from the one I knew in Milano. Perhaps you are right, Gideon. Perhaps if we two can between us discover some way to get him to go back to Milano, he will become the same old Bernardo again, and not *un cane grosso*—this big dog!''

She had, needless to say, succeeded in garnering Gideon's undivided attention. He sat up, running a hand through his hair. "Get him to go back to Italy? We could do that? But—but the Conte doesn't have any money!"

"*I* have money, *cugino*. *Nonno* has given me an allowance. I have one thousand pounds. We could give this to Bernardo. It is enough money, yes?"

Gideon's eyes all but burst out of their sockets. "Uncle Denny gave you *what?* Then it's true—he is dicked in the nob! His only nephew deep in dun territory, and he's giving *you* a thousand pounds to buy hair ribbons!" His eyes retreated back into his skull as his eyelids narrowed speculatively. "You wouldn't wish to make your dearest cousin a small loan, would you, Allegra? Say, ah, *half* your thousand?"

Allegra shook her head. "I am so sorry, Gideon. I know I should loan it to you, if just to make up for teasing you so with *Nonno*, but I cannot. I shall need it all for our passages, and until I am once more up on my toes in Italy.''

If Valerian had been privy to this conversation, he could have corrected Allegra by saying, ''You mean back on your feet, imp.'' Valerian might have said it, but it is doubtful that he would have done so. Instead, just as Gideon did now, he most probably would have exploded, ''*You're* going back to Italy!''

However, unlike Valerian's explosion into speech, which would have doubtless carried more than a hint of incredulity, Gideon's voice eloquently conveyed his elation—and his sudden and complete recovery from his latest ''illness.''

Allegra shrugged, her fingers idly stroking one of the rabbit's worn velvet ears. ''I have no choice, *cugino*. Italy is my real home. Much as I am grateful to *Nonno* for asking for me, I now know I can never be really happy here. But I will need help, Gideon, to sneak away.''

Gideon passed over Allegra's unhappiness without regret, concentrating on how this latest development would affect him. ''All right,'' he said, swinging his legs over the edge of the mattress—which was not all that shocking, since he had been lying fully clothed beneath the satin coverlet.

''Give me a minute to think this thing out. You wish to return to Italy. Where you go, the Conte goes. If you go, Uncle Denny's money reverts to Mama. If the Conte goes, Mama reverts to me. Isobel? Who cares where she goes?''

He snatched up the rabbit and began pacing the floor, rubbing the velvet animal's hide against his cheek. "I know. Isobel will sink into a sad decline. Yes, and Uncle Denny will go tripping back to the Pavilion to act the toadeater. Mama will once more get to handle the family purse strings, and I—ah! I get to live again! I can pay my debts and maybe even buy a half share of that racehorse Georgie told me about! A real goer, Georgie said."

He stopped and whirled about, pointing the rabbit at Allegra. "What about Valerian? Where does Fitzhugh come into this? Won't Uncle Denny just send him out to drag you back here, like some damned hound faithfully retrieving a stick?"

Allegra shook her head. "Valerian is finished with me. I am a graceless disgrace in his eyes. He will be too busy rejoicing over my absence to follow me. But that does not mean that he will like it even a little bit if he discovers that I am leaving, for he went to a great deal of trouble to deliver me here in the first place. Gideon—I must be on my way at once. It has been two days since Valerian was last here, and I know he will be back soon, when he thinks I am done with throwing things."

"You throw things?"

She hopped to her feet, wishing Gideon would keep his mind on the subject at hand. "Never mind, *cugino*. Are you going to help me or not? I would go to Isobel, who would dearly like to see the back of me, except that she believes herself so in love with Bernardo that she would perish before allowing him to return to Italy." She made a face. "Isobel is so nice to me now. She is so nice to me that I have lost all my appetite and cannot eat. When I think of Valerian and the fool I made of myself with him, I cannot eat. *Cugino,* you must help me, before I fade into a small nothingness!''

Gideon stood in the middle of the room, hugging the velvet rabbit to himself in glee. ''Help you, cousin? If you grow faint from hunger, why, I shall carry you aboard ship myself!''

MAX, ACTING AS Bernardo's interpreter, had been haunting the Dugdale house for the past two days, trying for a word alone with Allegra, but she had proved so elusive that he had nothing to report to an anxious Valerian when he and Bernardo returned that night to the Fitzhugh estate.

''Playing least in sight, that's what the little darlin' is doing,'' Max told Valerian when the two of them were finally alone, Bernardo having been tucked up in bed with a bowl of the sugarplums he favored (to be joined, unbeknownst to Valerian, not five minutes later by the Fitzhugh upstairs maidservant, who did not find her unfamiliarity with Italian to be an insurmountable barrier to a most intimate relationship with the handsome shoemaker).

''I don't like this, Max,'' Valerian said, downing the last of his brandy before refilling his glass from the decanter. ''She refuses to see me. She sends back my notes, unread. I can't get within ten feet of her. And Duggy—he's no help at all. Says Allegra is devoting herself to him. She's hiding from me, that's what she's doing!''

Max sat at his ease in the oak-paneled, study, his shrewd gaze concentrated on Valerian's face. ''And why would she be doin' that, I want to know. You wouldn't be tryin' anythin' nasty with the girl, would you? I had the two of you as good as wed.''

"And we would be, if I could only get the little imp to stay in one place long enough for me to propose to her properly!'' Valerian exploded, collapsing into the leather high-backed chair facing Max's. "Do you have any idea how difficult it is to propose marriage to a young lady who has already told you—at least twice—that you love her and wish to marry her? I feel as if I've been thrust headlong into a farce and Allegra has stolen all my lines!''

"Took the teeth right out of your saw, did she?'' Max took a deep drink of brandy. "Ah! Wonderful cellar you have, Valerian. Just like a torchlight procession going down my throat, don't you know. Now, to get back to your problem, boyo. The colleen has told you all about *you*. Has she told you all about *her*, I'm wonderin'?''

Valerian's head came up. "You mean, has she told me she loves me?'' He frowned, considering the question. "She allowed me to kiss her. She kissed me back.'' He shook his head, dismissing what he'd just said. "She also told me, while we were still in Italy, that she would never forgive me for sending her to the back door of my hotel—but that seems so long ago. Surely she didn't mean that.''

He looked worriedly at Max. "She wouldn't still be holding a grudge, and trying to pay me out the same way she tricked Gideon into asking Dugdale for her hand. And she couldn't really be angry with me for teasing her for all but asking me to propose to her. Could she?''

Max shrugged. ''I'm not the one wearin' this slipper, boyo. Don't ask *me* where it pinches.''

''You want me to ask Allegra if she loves me— *after* she let me kiss her? I can't do that. I might just as well accuse her of being a loose woman!'' Valerian collapsed against the back of the chair. ''You know, Max, I used to be considered a very intelligent, well-ordered man. Now my life is a shambles, and I cannot add two and two with any real hope of ending up with four. Is it love itself that causes this condition, or is it Allegra in particular? I vow, my life has been complete chaos since I met her. I cut short my travels, have dined with Prinny—which I vowed never to do—have a shoemaker turned Conte living under my roof, and am contemplating marriage to a woman who may either love me or be working some sort of bizarre Italian *vendetta* against me for rescuing her from poverty and that same shoemaker.''

Max lifted his glass in an impromptu toast ''To love! What a delightful muddle!'' He downed his drink, shivering as the brandy licked hotly at the back of his throat. ''Drink up, boyo, for it's a dry bed and a wet bottle you're needin' tonight, don't you know. Drink until you lose the will to think. It'll be time and enough tomorrow to go after that little colleen— and then don't take no for an answer!''

It wasn't a very original idea—and probably not even a very good one—but it was the only suggestion that appealed to Valerian at that moment. He raised his own glass and drank deep.

ALLEGRA HAD SPENT a sleepless night—or a "white night," as she described it to Betty—and refused her breakfast tray, unable to summon an appetite. The maid, who seemed to have developed a very real attachment to her unconventional mistress, clucked and scolded for the entire length of time it took Allegra to bathe and dress in one of her new morning gowns, and then, thankfully, left her alone.

Allegra desperately needed to be alone. She desperately needed to think. Not that she hadn't spent the entire night thinking, but this time she knew she had to apply herself to subjects other than how wonderful it felt to be in Valerian's arms, how thrilling his kisses were, how dear his angel wings were to her, and how she adored it when he smiled at her in that special way and called her his imp.

That sort of thinking had served only to make her cry into her pillow, and the time for tears had passed. She had put Gideon in charge of securing passage for her on a ship—and for the ridiculous Bernardo as well—and she must be ready to leave at a moment's notice. Somehow she must convey this news to the shoemaker, and then convince him that he had no future in Brighton.

"Which will be about as simple as threading a needle at midnight," she told her reflection as she peered into the mirror, noticing that she was developing the slightest smudging of bruised purple beneath her eyes. She pinched her cheeks, bringing color into them, knowing that Valerian would pick up very quickly on her wan appearance.

Valerian. She had to be gone before he arrived. He

had put up with her nonsense for more than two days, but she knew he would not be put off much longer, and she would rather die than have to listen while he explained yet again that politely brought-up young ladies do *not* ask gentlemen to propose to them.

If only she hadn't run from the room, unable to control the tears that had threatened to destroy her completely. If only she had stayed, challenging him to explain why a gentleman may kiss a young lady and then *not* propose to her!

Except then, of course, Valerian might have pointed out—as he had done in Italy when he had sent her around to the servants' entrance of the hotel—that she was not a politely brought-up young lady. Perhaps, in his eyes, she was still the barefoot, none-too-clean girl he had met in Florence, a desperate, out-of-work opera singer who had taken to stealing sausages.

No! He loved her! He had to love her! She was Allegra Crispino, singer. She had even sung before the next King of England—and everyone had loved her! She must never forget that night. She must take it to her heart and treasure it always!

Allegra reluctantly quit her room, to wander aimlessly through the house and out into the back garden, where she had promised to meet with Gideon as soon as he returned from booking passage on a ship to Italy.

She took up a seat beneath a tree that was just beginning to bud and deliberately began humming snatches from the aria she had sung at the Pavilion, in the hope that it would improve her mood.

"That sounds familiar," Valerian said, walking up behind her so quietly that she was startled into silence. "Listen, imp. Even the birds in the trees cannot help but sing along with you."

"Valerian!" Allegra's eyes widened in panic. "I didn't expect...well, I guess I did expect...although I had hoped to be...but you are early." She deliberately avoided meeting his eyes, looking past him toward the door to the drawing room. "Is—is Bernardo with you?"

"Well, now, imp, thereby hangs a tale." Valerian sat down beside her on the bench, his lips twitching in amusement. "No, Bernardo is not with me. You see, the Conte Timoteo is aboard *The Valiant Lady*, already bound for Naples, several thousand pounds richer than he was upon his arrival in Brighton, and very happy to be seeing the last of England."

Allegra knew her eyes had grown wide as saucers. "He is? But why? He seemed to be enjoying himself most mightily."

"Not entirely. Did you know, dearest girl, that Isobel tried to corner him yesterday in the Baron's morning room? Oh, yes, she did, and quite a sight that must have been. Bernardo was highly insulted—saying something about not being stuck twice by a large-toothed, chicken-breasted Englishwoman who wanted only to keep him on a leash. I believe he is planning to return to Milan and his family, with plans to enlarge their shop. It seems he has some new idea for boots with colored linings. Max went with him, eager to get back to Naples, but he leaves you his love and the wish that you may visit him soon."

Allegra couldn't help herself. She looked up, straight into Valerian's eyes, and burst into delighted laughter. Totally forgetting herself, she then fell against Valerian's shoulder, mirth mingled with relief all but overcoming her, and it wasn't until several moments had passed that she realized he had put his arms around her and was holding her close against his chest.

"Valerian?" she questioned, reluctantly pushing herself free of his embrace. "I am correct in thinking that well-brought-up young ladies do not laugh quite so heartily—or do not do so in a gentleman's arms— yes? I am yet again a disgrace to you."

He pulled her to him once more, lifting her chin with the tip of one finger. "A nuisance, yes. A maddening, confusing, adorable bundle of hot emotions, yes. But a disgrace, Allegra? When have you ever been a disgrace?"

Allegra could have begun listing the times she had behaved badly, counting them off on her fingers for him—beginning with her outrageous behavior in Italy and ending with her overweening arrogance in assuming that he loved her and then telling him so—but she decided against it.

After all, Valerian was with her now, and he was looking at her in that special way, a look that had once confused but now thrilled her. She was in his arms, Bernardo was gone from the scene, and it appeared that, yet again, she had landed on her toes.

This was not the time to tempt fate by reminding him of things best placed in *dimenticatoio*—that lovely, wholly imaginary place in which to put forgotten things.

And to think she had planned to leave England without ever seeing him again, while still harboring the desperate hope that he would posthaste come chasing after her once more, begging her to love him. But then he wasn't to know that, was he? Nobody was to know that except for her—she with her temperamental Crispino and devious Dugdale blood running hot in her veins—and *she* certainly wasn't going to tell him!

Valerian tipped Allegra's head to one side and began nibbling very delicately at the base of her throat, sending a shiver delicately through her. Was this the reaction of a man who did not love her? Was this the reaction of a man who wanted nothing more than to be a good friend to her grandfather by keeping her out of mischief, while at the same time wishing that he could be shed of her once and for all?

This was wonderful. This was everything she had ever hoped for, and she hadn't had to run all the way back to Italy to know once and for all that Valerian loved her. She had only to sit in the back garden of Number 23, and love had come to her.

She raised a hand to cup his cheek, her head thrown back as his lips traced a path from her throat to the corner of her mouth. "You were going to say something to me the other day, Valerian, something I did not think I wished to hear. Now I wonder if I made yet another mistake. Perhaps you will tell me now, while I am so very much interested in listening."

But now Valerian wasn't listening. The feel of her,

the scent of her, the taste of her, had driven all rational thought from his mind. Talk? Who wished to talk when there were so many more delightful things they could be doing? There was plenty of time for talk. They had a lifetime to talk.

She was here. She was in his arms, willingly, happily, in his arms. She wasn't the mercurial Allegra now, the one-moment hot, one-moment cold bundle of conflicting emotions that so excited him, yet so confused him.

How could he ever have thought she had only been boasting that he loved her—much in the way she had boasted about her voice, and how she *had* sung for the Bishop of Bologna? She *did* have the most glorious, pure voice he had ever heard. She had sung for the Bishop—for the next King of England as well! Allegra didn't boast. Allegra merely told the truth— except for those times when she bent it a little to suit her own purpose. But then, bless her, what woman didn't?

"Valerian? You will tell me—"

He silenced her with his mouth, his kiss shattering all thought as they melted together on the bench in the back garden of Number 23, oblivious to the world around them…the birds singing above them in the budding branches of the tree…the sound of the door to the drawing room opening…the footfalls that should have alerted them to the fact that they were no longer alone.

"Excuse me, Fitzhugh," Gideon announced with obvious glee. "I hate to be the one to throw a damper on what appears to be a touching moment, but—"

Valerian pushed Allegra's face protectively against his chest, not ready to relinquish his hold on her, and looked daggers at the younger man, who was standing directly in front of them, grinning like the cat that has cornered the mouse. ''Nonsense, Kittredge. Don't hold back—not when you do it so very well.''

Allegra stiffened, feeling the animosity sparkling between the two men, then began to tremble as she realized that, just when she thought her world had turned rosy, all her carelessly loosed pigeons were about to come home to roost. Allegra had never underestimated Gideon—not when she had first met him in the Dugdale drawing room, and not now. He had seen her and Valerian together, and had instantly understood everything. She struggled to get free, anxious to keep Gideon from speaking, but Valerian continued to hold her close.

Gideon knew now that he had *never* had a chance with Allegra. She had most definitely been leading him on, just as he had told her, so that he could debase himself in front of his uncle, who would then ring a mighty peal over his head. He was still not too clear on why she had come to him for help—perhaps she'd also at some point taken a pet against Fitzhugh that had now been resolved—but it was definitely clear to him that he had been made a cat's paw of yet again.

She had roused him from his bed of pain, sending him off to procure passage for her and that Italian popinjay, only to snuggle up with Fitzhugh, who, unless he missed his guess, would soon be the possessor of both the promised plum and Allegra's eventual inheritance.

Gone was his hope of regaining his share of the Dugdale fortune. Equally fled were his chances of paying his debts and buying part of Georgie's racehorse. And, to put the capper on it, that insufferable Conte would remain underfoot, to blight him with his beauty.

Gideon realized that he was beginning to breathe very quickly, his shallow breaths causing him to feel slightly light-headed. Perhaps he should seek out his mother, and have her monitor his racing pulse. But no! First he would destroy his cousin, this maddening Italian interloper in his once well-cushioned life, for now and for all time!

He stepped forward another pace and smiled down at Allegra, who was, he noticed, looking decidedly pale. "I have the tickets and passports you asked me to procure for you, dearest cousin. You and the Conte can take ship tonight and leave on the morning tide. Here," he concluded triumphantly, flinging a small packet into her lap. *"Bon voyage!"*

Allegra watched as Gideon, walking with a definite spring in his step, returned to the house, leaving her alone with Valerian, whose arms had deserted her halfway through her cousin's speech, leaving her to shiver in the sudden chill that had invaded the air.

"I—I suppose you would like to hear some sort of explanation?" she suggested at last, when the silence had become unbearable.

"Not really," Valerian answered evenly, rising to stand in front of her. "I think I'd rather work this one out for myself. You were perhaps planning to escort Bernardo back to Milan before he could father an entire generation of beautiful, dull-witted Adonises here in Brighton? Oh, yes, I may have forgotten to tell you, imp, but it seems your once devoted swain has recovered from his heartbreak with a vengeance. Max found him this morning with not one but two of my housemaids in his—well, never mind that.

"Passing over that idea," he went on, his heart growing, "I would have to believe that you were planning not to escort Bernardo but to *accompany* him back to Italy. You would do this because you are desperately unhappy here in Brighton. Now, as you have mastered the Kittredges, and as you have grown extremely fond of Duggy—though I still cannot bring myself to understand why—and you have become a great sensation here in Brighton, I can only deduce that you had felt it necessary to run away from someone or something."

"Valerian, I—"

"Hush, imp, and let me finish. Yes, you were running away. Now, whom have you been avoiding these past days? Why, I do believe it is I—am I correct? You have been avoiding me. Is this because you cannot stand the sight of me? Modesty to one side, I don't think so. Is it possibly because you feel you have made a spectacle of yourself merely by being—bless you—yourself? Ah, now this has the ring of typical Allegra Crispino logic. Max told me a woman's mind is a curious thing, but you, my love—and almost always for what you believe to be the best of reasons—have turned chaos into an art form."

"Valerian! I—"

He looked down at her, reaching out his hands to pull her to her feet. "If we really work at it, imp, I suppose we could go round and round for several days—or even months—trying to explain to each other all that has transpired since first we met. But that would be very fatiguing, and not at all sensible, don't you agree?"

He was actually asking for her opinion? He had finally done with spouting absurdities, his handsome, adorable face split in an unholy grin. Allegra opened her mouth to speak. "Valerian, I—"

But he cut her off once again. "Don't say another word, my darling. Just listen. I don't care why you thought you had to flee, since you aren't going anywhere ever again without me by your side. You don't have to say anything because you have already said it all. I love you. Everyone loves you. It's impossible not to, imp. And yes, I want to marry you. *Now* you may speak. Are you going to become my wife, Allegra, or am I going to spend the rest of my life chasing after you with twice the perseverance and determination of a dozen Bernardo Timoteos?"

She smiled at him, her heart and her love shining in her tear-bright sapphire eyes, then said cheekily, "I will give you my answer very soon, dearest Valerian, but first, I think I should like for us to adjourn to the kitchens for something to eat. Suddenly I find myself *very* hungry!"

EPILOGUE

THE CHARITY PERFORMANCE at the Theatre Royal, complete with the Prince Regent in attendance, had been a triumph, although Allegra Crispino Fitzhugh got no closer to the stage than her seat of honor beside Prinny in his private box.

Isobel, the original architect of the scheme, who had conceived such a performance as the scene of Allegra's ultimate disgrace, had not been present as several very talented singers gathered by Valerian performed to raise funds for the widows and orphans of soldiers who had died in the war. Isobel, along with her mother and brother, had removed to Wolverhampton the previous week on a "repairing lease" that was to last as long as Baron Dugdale desired— since it was he who, only when he was good and ready, would ultimately pay his nephew's gaming debts so that the Kittredges could again show their faces in Brighton without the danger of Gideon being set upon by his angry creditors.

"Best stretch of peace and quiet I've had since Aggie and her brats moved in," he had told Valerian happily as he waved the newly wed couple on their way after the performance and made to join the Prince Regent for a late supper at the Pavilion.

Allegra was still singing snatches from one of the arias that had been performed as Valerian entered their bedchamber an hour later, already dressed in his nightclothes, a burgundy banyan tied about his trim waist.

He looked at his wife of three weeks, happy to see that she was still clothed in the pearled-petal-strewn gown that would always be a reminder of the day he had completely and totally lost his heart to her. How he would delight in divesting her of it.

"Imp?" he prompted, interrupting her as she whirled about the room, holding up her skirts delicately while she sang another verse in lilting Italian.

"Valerian!" Allegra immediately broke off her song to launch herself into his outstretched arms. "Ah, *caro mio,* what a night! You did not mind that Prinny pinched me, yes? It was only the once, and he was so good to allow the performance. And you did once say that you felt sorry for him."

Valerian frowned as he steered her toward the wide bed, for he had missed the pinch. "Not *that* sorry, imp. Now sit down, my darling, for I have something to tell you."

"A surprise? Oh, how lovely!" Allegra's sapphire eyes shone brightly as she scrambled to the very center of the bed, her ivory taffeta skirts billowing around her. She patted the space next to her, inviting him to join her. "But you must be careful not to muss my gown. I have told Betty you would act as my maid tonight, and she would not like it if this pretty thing were to become a mass of wrinkles."

Valerian ignored the warning, watching, entranced,

as Allegra contradicted herself by collapsing against
the pillows, then lay close against her on his side, his
head propped on his hand. It was difficult to keep his
mind on what he wished to say when Allegra began
running her fingertips up and down his bare forearm,
but he did his best. "How would you like to go back
to Italy, imp?" he asked, observing the pearled petals
flutter invitingly with her every breath.

"Italia?" Allegra's smooth brow furrowed in confusion. "I thought you wished to open the London
house for what you called the Season. You have
changed your mind? Why?"

Valerian's left hand reached out to begin idly playing with one of the pearled petals on her bodice. "I
had a dream last night, imp," he said, his voice
slightly husky. "In my dream we were installed in a
villa on Capri, just the two of us, spending lazy days
visiting Roman ruins and the grottoes and long, wonderful nights lying in a glorious, gauze-hung bedchamber, visiting the stars."

"Visiting the stars?" Allegra's smile was of wonder. "I think you must show me how we did that,
caro mio, for I am not sure if I know what you
mean."

He leaned across her body, pushing himself up on
his elbows, his face mere inches from hers. "I think
you know, imp. You know very well." His lips teas-
ingly brushed hers. "*Amerò* my darling. I will love."

She reached up a hand to brush at his beloved angel
wings, then traced the line of his cheek. "Ah, Valerian. *Amerai*—you will love. I like that. And then?"

He briefly turned his lips into her palm, then looked

deeply into her eyes and whispered, "And then, my dearest imp, *ameremo*—we will love."

"*Amiamo, caro mio*—we love!" Allegra agreed, willingly surrendering her lips to his.

And then there was no more need for words.

Every day is

A Mother's Day

in this heartwarming anthology
celebrating motherhood and romance!

Featuring the classic story "Nobody's Child" by Emilie Richards
He had come to a child's rescue, and now Officer Farrell Riley was
suddenly sharing parenthood with beautiful Gemma Hancock.
But would their ready-made family last forever?

Plus two brand-new romances:

"Baby on the Way" by Marie Ferrarella
Single and pregnant, Madeline Reed found the perfect husband in the
handsome cop who helped bring her infant son into the world. But did his
dutiful role in the surprise delivery make J. T. Walker a daddy?

"A Daddy for Her Daughters" by Elizabeth Bevarly
When confronted with spirited Naomi Carmichael and her brood of girls,
bachelor Sloan Sullivan realized he had a lot to learn about women!
Especially if he hoped to win this sexy single mom's heart....

Available this April from Silhouette Books!

COOPER'S  CORNER

In April 2002 you are invited to three wonderful weddings in a very special town...

A Wedding at Cooper's Corner

USA Today **bestselling author**

Kristine Rolofson
Muriel Jensen
Bobby Hutchinson

Ailing Warren Cooper has asked private investigator David Solomon to deliver three precious envelopes to each of his grandchildren. Inside each is something that will bring surprise, betrayal...and unexpected romance!

And look for the exciting launch of *Cooper's Corner,* a NEW 12-book continuity from Harlequin— launching in August 2002.

HARLEQUIN®
Makes any time special ®

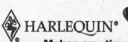

MONTANA *Born*

From the bestselling series

MONTANA MAVERICKS

Wed in Whitehorn

Two tales that capture living and loving
beneath the Big Sky.

THE MARRIAGE MAKER by Christie Ridgway

Successful businessman Ethan Redford never proposed a deal he
couldn't close—and that included marriage to Cleo Kincaid Monroe!

AND THE WINNER...WEDS! by Robin Wells

Prim and proper Frannie Hannon yearned for Austin Parker, but
her pearls and sweater sets couldn't catch his boots and jeans—or
could they?

And don't miss

MONTANA *Bred*

Featuring

JUST PRETENDING by Myrna Mackenzie

&

STORMING WHITEHORN by Christine Scott

Available in May 2002
Available only from Silhouette at your favorite retail outlet.

Silhouette
Where love comes alive

Visit Silhouette at www.eHarlequin.com   PSBORN

These New York Times *bestselling authors*
have created stories to capture the hearts and minds
of women everywhere.
Here are three classic tales about the power of love—
and the wonder of discovering the place
where you belong....

FINDING HOME

DUNCAN'S BRIDE
by
LINDA HOWARD

CHAIN LIGHTNING
by
ELIZABETH LOWELL

POPCORN AND KISSES
by
KASEY MICHAELS

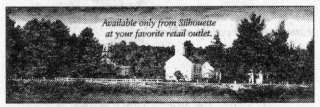

Silhouette Romance introduces tales of
enchanted love and things beyond explanation
in the new series

Soulmates

Couples destined for each other are brought
together by the powerful magic of love....

A precious gift brings
A HUSBAND IN HER EYES
by Karen Rose Smith (on sale March 2002)

Dreams come true in
CASSIE'S COWBOY
by Diane Pershing (on sale April 2002)

A legacy of love arrives
BECAUSE OF THE RING
by Stella Bagwell (on sale May 2002)

*Available at
your favorite retail outlet.*

Where love comes alive™

Visit Silhouette at www.eHarlequin.com
SRSOUL